Victor Meunier

Adventures of the Great Hunting Grounds of the World

Victor Meunier

Adventures of the Great Hunting Grounds of the World

ISBN/EAN: 9783742813787

Manufactured in Europe, USA, Canada, Australia, Japa

Cover: Foto ©Andreas Hilbeck / pixelio.de

Manufactured and distributed by brebook publishing software
(www.brebook.com)

Victor Meunier

Adventures of the Great Hunting Grounds of the World

ADVENTUR[ES]

ON THE

GREAT HUNTING G[ROUNDS]

OF THE WORLD.

By VICTOR MEUNIER.

Illustrated with Twenty-two Woodcuts.

NEW YORK:

CHARLES SCRIBNER & CO.

1870.

Illustrated Library of Wonders.

PUBLISHED BY

Messrs. Charles Scribner & Co.,

654 BROADWAY, NEW YORK.

Each one volume 12mo.   Price per volume, $1.50

Titles of Books.	No. of Illustrations.
THUNDER AND LIGHTNING,	39
WONDERS OF OPTICS,	70
WONDERS OF HEAT,	90
INTELLIGENCE OF ANIMALS,	54
GREAT HUNTS,	22
EGYPT 3,300 YEARS AGO,	40
WONDERS OF POMPEII,	22
THE SUN, BY A. GUILLEMIN,	58
SUBLIME IN NATURE,	50
WONDERS OF GLASS-MAKING,	63
WONDERS OF ITALIAN ART,	28
WONDERS OF THE HUMAN BODY,	45
WONDERS OF ARCHITECTURE,	50
LIGHTHOUSES AND LIGHTSHIPS,	60
BOTTOM OF THE OCEAN,	68
* WONDERS OF BODILY STRENGTH AND SKILL,	70
* WONDERFUL BALLOON ASCENTS,	30
ACOUSTICS,	114
* WONDERS OF THE HEAVENS,	48
* THE MOON, BY A. GUILLEMIN,	60
* WONDERS OF SCULPTURE,	61
* WONDERS OF ENGRAVING,	32
* WONDERS OF VEGETATION,	45
* WONDERS OF THE INVISIBLE WORLD,	97
* CELEBRATED ESCAPES,	26
* WATER,	77
* HYDRAULICS,	40
* ELECTRICITY,	71
* SUBTERRANEAN WORLD,	27

* In Press for early Publication.

The above works sent to any address, post-paid, upon receipt of the price by the publishers.

The object which the Compiler has had in view in producing the following work, has been to present to the young reader a collection of well-authenticated facts, illustrative of the nature, habits, and various modes of capturing some of the largest and fiercest of the animal world, and to describe some of the numerous adventures, terrible fights, and hairbreadth escapes which the hunting of these animals has given rise to. For this purpose M. Victor Meunier has availed himself of the writings of a great variety of travellers of different countries, ancient as well as modern; and in thus bringing together their varied and often conflicting statements, he has endeavoured, without entering into minute scientific details, to bring them into harmony, or to arrive at the truth on disputed points.

The Translator, notwithstanding the temptation which an almost inexhaustible field presented to him of adding illustration and adventure, has confined himself, with one or two exceptions, to an almost literal translation of M. Victor Meunier's compilation. To the chapters on Elephants he has appended a very interesting account of the Duke of Edinburgh's Elephant Hunt in South Africa. This account he has ventured to give, not only because it records the latest, but perhaps the only hunt of the kind in which a Royal prince of England has ever been engaged, at least in recent times, and not the less so on account of the real pluck and spirit, characteristic of his race, which the adventure called forth in him.

In the chapter on Crocodiles an extract is also given from a work just published by Don Ramon Paez, entitled, "Travels and Adventures in South and Central America," which will not be found in the original French work.

E. M.

CONTENTS.

CHAPTER I.

CHAPTER II.

CHAPTER III.

CHAPTER IV.

CHAPTER V.

PAGE

CHAPTER VI.

CHAPTER VII.

CHAPTER VIII.

CHAPTER IX.

CHAPTER X.

CHAPTER XI.

CHAPTER XII.

CHAPTER XIII.

CHAPTER XIV.

CHAPTER XV.

CHAPTER XVI.

CHAPTER XVII.

LIST OF ILLUSTRATIONS.

CHAPTER I.

𝕿𝖍𝖊 𝕲𝖔𝖗𝖎𝖑𝖑𝖆.

I.—Stories of Travellers.

For three centuries the rumour has been current that there existed on the western coast of Africa, north and south of the equator, an ape of immense strength and gigantic size,—of all animals the largest and most formidable—the king of the African forests.

Let us see what travellers say concerning this animal.

At the beginning of the seventeenth century Andrew Battel, who had been for a long time a prisoner of the Portuguese in Angola, described, under the name of *Pongo*, an ape resembling a man in all his proportions, but as large as a giant, and so strong that ten men were not sufficient to subdue one of them.

"He has a human face," said Battel, "with sunken eyes, long hair on the sides of his head, his face naked, as well as his ears and his hands; his body rather shaggy; his hair of dark brown. He differs from

B

man in outward appearance chiefly in having little or
no calves to his legs. Nevertheless, he walks upright,
holding his hands clasped behind his neck He sleeps
in trees, and constructs for himself a shelter against
the sun and rain; he lives on fruits; he cannot talk,
although he has a better understanding than other
animals. When travellers abandon, in the morning,
the fire which they have kept during the night, the
pongoes come and sit around it until it becomes extinct,
but they have not sufficient intelligence to gather wood
to keep it alive. They go in companies, they kill the
negroes they encounter; they will even attack an elephant, and put him to flight by blows with their fists
or with sticks."

Bosman, another traveller in Guinea, has spoken
of the same ape. "They grow extremely large," he
wrote; "I have seen one with my own eyes which was
five feet high; they have a very ugly figure, are very
wicked, very bold, and sufficiently daring to attack
men. Some negroes assure us that these apes
can talk, and that if they don't do so, it is
because they don't wish to give themselves the
trouble. It would perhaps be better to say that they
are capable of understanding all one would wish to
teach them."

M. de la Brosse, in a journey on the coast of
Angola, published in 1738, says that they attain the

height of six and seven feet, that their strength is without equal, that they live in huts, and use clubs to defend themselves. He thus describes them :—

"Face dull, nose snubbed and flat, ears without cushions, skin a little lighter than that of a mulatto, hair long and thin on many parts of the body, stomach extremely tight, the heels flat, and elevated about half an inch at the back. They walk on two feet, and on all-fours when they have the fancy to do so." M. de la Brosse adds that they endeavour to carry off the negresses, keep them with them, and treat them very well. "I have known at Lowango a negress who had been three years with these animals."

Finally, Mr. Bowditch, in his "Narrative of a Mission from Cape Coast Castle to Ashantee" (London, 1819), writes :—

"The favourite and most curious subject of our conversation on natural history was the *Ingéna*, an animal like the orang-outang, but of a much greater size, being five feet in height and four feet across the shoulders. Its paw was said to be still more disproportionate, and one blow of it would cause death. Travellers who go to Kaybe frequently encounter him. He lies in ambush to kill passers-by, and he principally feeds on wild honey. Among other traits which characterize this animal, and on which all persons agree, it is reported that he builds for himself a hut, in rude imitation of that of the natives, and that he sleeps outside on the roof of this dwelling.

It is needless to say that Africa does not contain an ape which bears resemblance to man in all his proportions, and which differs from him exteriorly only in the small protuberance of his calves, and who does not talk simply because he does not wish to give himself the trouble. "I regret," says an author, from whom presently we shall frequently borrow,—"I regret to be obliged to destroy agreeable illusions; but the gorilla does not lie in ambush behind trees to seize with his claws the defenceless traveller. He does not strangle him between his feet as in a vice; he does not carry away women from their villages; he does not build for himself a hut of branches in the forests; he does not march in troops, and in all that has been said of his attacks *en masse*, there is not the shadow of truth."

The reports of travellers were then imbued with exaggerations and errors; but beyond what was erroneous and improbable, these accounts agree in attesting the existence of an ape distinct from the chimpanzee, larger, stronger, and more dangerous than this latter, and of that there was no reason to doubt.

Attention was then aroused to the subject. It was in 1846 that all doubts ceased.

It happened that at that period an American missionary, the Rev. Dr. J. Leighton Wilson, discovered at the Gaboon the skull of a new and extraordinary kind of ape. A narrow cranial cavity, almost wholly behind the orbits of the eyes, and where the cerebral convolutions had left but feeble impression; jaw-bones of prodigious power, projecting in front, and armed with formidable and deeply rooted tusks; at the extremities of the eyebrows, on the line of the parietal bones, and at the junction of these with the occipital, were enormous bony ridges; finally, very large and arched cheek-bones: in a word, all the characters of bestiality carried to excess and united to those of strength without equal among apes: such was this skull, which could only have belonged to the *Ingéna* of Bowditch, to the *Pongo* of Battel. A learned American naturalist, Professor Jeffries Wyman, gave a description of it in 1847 in the " Journal of Natural History of Boston." The discovery of Mr. Wilson did not long remain isolated, and the anatomy of the new quadrumane, to which Wilson had given the name of *Gorilla*, became the object of the labours of Richard Owen in England, of Isidore Geoffroy Saint Hilaire and of Duvernoy in France. The interest still increased when the first white man who had seen a living gorilla face to face had made known his marvellous stories of the chase.

This white man is an American of French origin, M. Paul du Chaillu.

He embarked, in the month of October, 1855, for the western coast of Africa. His intention was to devote some years to the exploration of the region comprised between two degrees North and two degrees South latitude over the whole space which extends from the coast to the chain of mountains called the Sierra del Crystal. This country is the domain of the gorilla. Many times, during a former excursion in Africa, our traveller had heard of this animal, of his terrible roar, his prodigious strength, and great courage. To reach the gorilla in his haunts, to kill him, and so to enrich science, was one of the objects which M. du Chaillu had in view. We are going to see him at the work.

But whilst he is seeking this extraordinary being, let us listen to the stories told by the negroes whilst sitting round their camp fires, as reported by the American author.

II.—Stories of the Negroes.

"My father," said one, "used to relate, that being one day in the forest, he suddenly found himself face to face with a great gorilla, which barred the way. My father held his lance in his hand; at sight of this weapon the gorilla began to roar. Then my father, frightened, let fall his lance. When the gorilla saw that he was disarmed, he seemed satisfied; he looked at him for an instant, and then left him and returned into the depths of the forest. My father, on his side, was well content, and pursued his journey."

And the auditors cried with one voice, "Yes, yes, that's it; when you meet a gorilla, let fall your lance, and you will appease him!"

"Some dry seasons since," said another, "a man, after a violent quarrel, disappeared from my village. A short time afterwards an Ashira, going into the forest, met there a very large gorilla. This gorilla was the man himself who had disappeared. He leapt on the poor Ashira, bit a piece of flesh from his arm, and then allowed him to go. The unfortunate man returned with his arm all bleeding, and told me of his adventure. I hope we shall not encounter any of these man-gorillas, for they are very wicked beings, and we shall have a terrible time of it."

The chorus replied, "No, no, we shall not meet with these wicked gorillas!"

"They believe, in fact," says the author already quoted, "that there are some gorillas of a particular kind which serve as the habitation of the spirits of certain dead negroes. The initiated recognize them by mysterious signs, and, above all, by their extraordinary stature. These gorillas, according to the Indians, can never be taken or killed; they have also more sagacity

and reason than the common animals. In these possessed beasts the intelligence of man is united with
the strength and ferocity of the animal.

"Some years ago a man disappeared, carried off
probably by a tiger. It was said, and believed, that
one day, whilst he was walking in the woods, he had
been metamorphosed into a hideous gorilla, which the
blacks had often pursued without being able to kill,
although he continually haunted the outskirts of the
village."

Here is another story:—

Some natives encountered, in a field of sugar-canes,
a troop of gorillas tying up the canes in bundles to carry
them away. They attacked them, but the apes put
them to flight, and they lost many men, some killed,
others prisoners. A few days after, the latter returned
home with their finger and toe-nails torn off.

Two Mbondémos women were walking in a forest,
when suddenly an enormous gorilla bestrode the path,
and seizing one of the women, carried her off, in spite
of her efforts and her cries. The other, trembling with
terror, returned to the village and related the adventure.

Naturally, her companion was held as lost. What
was the general surprise when, at the end of a few
days, she returned home!

"It was a gorilla possessed by a spirit," cried one
of the hearers.

A gorilla was walking in the forest, when he met a leopard. Both stood still. The quadruped, which was hungry, drew himself up to make a. spring at the throat of his enemy, who immediately commenced a fearful howling. Without allowing himself to be intimidated, the leopard took his leap; as ill luck would have it, he was caught in the air by the gorilla, who seized him by the tail, and twisted it round and round with such force that it came off, and the animal fled, leaving his appendage in the hands of the gorilla.

Returned to his comrades, the quadruped had to reply to their questions.

"What has happened?" they asked him. It was necessary to tell the whole story, at which news the king of the leopards howled so long and so strong, that from all points of the forest his subjects came together. Hardly had they learnt the injury done to their brother, than they swore to revenge it, and at once they entered the field in pursuit of the gorilla.

Their search did not last long. As soon as the great ape saw them approach, he tore up a tree, and using it as a club, he whirled it round with an air so menacing, that he held in abeyance the army of his assailants; but at last he grew tired, seeing which, the leopards rushed upon him altogether, and strangled him.

One day, another gorilla was walking out in the forest with his wife and little boy, when he found himself suddenly *vis-à-vis* with an immense elephant, who said to him,—

"Let me pass, gorilla, for these forests belong to me."

"Oh, oh!" said the gorilla, "how do these forests belong to thee? Am I not the master here? Am I not the man of the woods?" So saying, he ordered his wife and his little boy to stand aside. He then broke off a large branch of a tree, and arming himself with it, he so belaboured the elephant that he was killed by his blows, and some days afterwards the carcase of the elephant was found on the ground, and the club lying beside him.

One fact believed by all the tribes who know a little of the gorilla is, that this animal conceals himself on the lower branches of trees, and that when any one passes his ambuscade, he seizes the unhappy wretch with his large and powerful hands, lifts him into the tree, and quietly chokes him.

They are quite persuaded that if a woman about to become a mother, or if only the husband of the woman should see a gorilla, or even a dead gorilla, the woman will give birth not to an infant, but to a little gorilla! "I have remarked this superstition," says M. du Chaillu, "amongst all the tribes, and only *à propos* of the gorilla."

But this superstition does not prevent them from

eating the gorilla. They carefully set apart the brains to make magic charms. "If we kill a gorilla to-morrow," said a black, "I should like to have a part of his brains for *fétiche.*" Nothing can render a man more intrepid than having a gorilla's brains for *fétiche.* "Yes," repeated the other, "that gives heart for every danger."

III.—On the Hunting Ground.

ACCOMPANIED by men and women of the tribe of Mbon-démos, M. du Chaillu, ascending the second range of the Sierra del Crystal, at length came upon an open space of ground, not far from the sources of the Ntambonny, where once had been established a Mbon-démo village. A degenerate kind of sugar-cane was growing where the houses had once stood. Tormented by hunger, the traveller had hastened to gather some of the stalks, but his men drew his attention to a cir-cumstance which gave quite a new turn to his ideas. Here and there the cane was beaten down, torn up by the roots, and lying about in fragments, which had evidently been chewed. The Mbondémos looked at each other in silence, and muttered, "*Njéna!*" that is to say, "Gorilla."

They were, in fact, traces of gorillas, and traces, too, quite fresh. They soon found the tracks of their feet, and there must have been four or five in the company. From time to time they had sat down to masticate the canes.

"It was the first time I had ever seen these foot-prints," writes M. du Chaillu, "and my sensations were indescribable. Here was I, now, it seemed, on the point of meeting face to face that monster of whose ferocity, strength, and cunning the natives had told me so much; an animal scarce known to the civilized world, and which no white man before had hunted. My heart beat till I feared its loud pulsations would alarm the gorilla, and my feelings were really excited to a painful degree.

"The women were terrified, poor things, and we left them a good escort of two or three men to take care of them and reassure them. Then the rest of us looked once more carefully at our guns, and the hunt began.

"We descended a hill, crossed a stream on a fallen log, and presently approached some huge boulders of granite. Alongside of this granite block lay an immense dead tree, and about this we saw many evi-dences of the very recent presence of the gorillas.

"Doubtless they were hiding behind these granite blocks, which it was necessary to surround. The hunters divided into two parties, one taking the right, the other the left, with guns cocked and in hand. The excitement of the blacks was even greater than that of their master. They advanced through the brushwood, which was dense and sombre, though it was broad day. Unfortunately, the circle had been too much enlarged. The watchful gorillas saw the hunters. Suddenly a strange discordant, half-human devilish cry arose, and they beheld four young gorillas running towards the deep forests. With their heads bent down, and their bodies stooping, they gave the idea of men who were flying for their lives. They resembled to a frightful degree hairy men.

" I protest," continues M. du Chaillu, " I felt almost like a murderer when I saw the gorillas this first time. Take with this their awful cry, which, fierce and animal as it is, has yet something human in its discordance, and you will cease to wonder that the natives have the wildest superstitions about these *wild men of the woods*. They all fired at once, but hit nothing ; then the hunters rushed on in pursuit : they ran until they were exhausted, but in vain. The alert beasts knew the woods better than their enemies, and so made good their escape."

So far, then, it was a failure ; but at least M. du Chaillu could boast of having seen living gorillas, and he lost no time in endeavouring to see them again, and more closely.

Some days after this fruitless hunt, the intrepid traveller and his friends the Mbondémos, starting early in the morning, explored for many hours the thickets and least approachable parts of the forest, but without finding the faintest trace of a gorilla, when suddenly one of the men uttered a little " *cluck* " with his tongue, which is the native's way of showing that something is stirring, and at the same time M. du Chaillu thought he heard—seemingly ahead of him—the noise as of some one breaking down the branches or twigs of trees. " This was the gorilla, I knew at once, by the eager and satisfied looks of the men.

" They looked once more carefully at their guns, to see if by any chance the powder had fallen out of the pans ; I also examined mine, to make sure that all was right ; and then we marched on cautiously. The singular noise of the breaking of tree branches continued ; we walked with the greatest care, making no noise at all. The countenances of the men showed that they thought themselves engaged in a very serious undertaking ; but we pushed on, until finally we thought we saw through the thick woods the moving of the branches and small trees, which the great beast was tearing down, probably to get from them the berries and fruits he lives on.

" Suddenly, as we were yet creeping along, in a silence which made a heavy breath seem loud and distinct, the woods were at once filled with the tremendous barking roar of the gorilla.

᠁ Then the underbrush swayed rapidly just ahead, and presently before us stood an immense male gorilla. He had gone through the jungle on all-fours, but when he saw our party he erected himself and looked us boldly in the face. He stood about a dozen yards from us, and was a sight I think I shall never forget. Nearly six feet high (he proved four inches shorter), with immense body, huge chest, and great muscular arms, with fiercely glaring large deep grey eyes, and a hellish expression of face, which seemed to me like some nightmare vision. Thus stood before us the king of the African forests.

" He was not afraid of us; he stood there and beat his breast with his huge fists till it resounded like an immense drum (its usual mode of offering defiance), meantime giving vent to roar after roar.

" The roar of the gorilla is the most singular and awful noise heard in these African woods. It begins with a sharp bark, like an angry dog, then glides into a deep bass roll, which literally and closely resembles the roll of distant thunder along the sky, for which I have sometimes been tempted to take it when I did not see the animal. So deep is it, that it seems to proceed less from the mouth and throat than from the deep chest and vast paunch.

" His eyes began to flash fiercer fire as we stood motionless on the defensive, and the crest of short hair which stands on his forehead began to twitch rapidly up and down, while his powerful fangs were shown as he sent forth a thunderous roar; and now truly he reminded me of nothing but some hellish dream-creature, a being of that hideous order—half man, half beast, which we find pictured by old artists in some representations of the infernal regions. He advanced a few steps, then stopped to utter that hideous roar again; advanced again, and finally stopped when at a distance of about six yards from us; and here, just as he began another of his roars, beating his breast in rage, we fired and killed him.

"With a groan, which had something terribly human in it, and yet was full of brutishness, he fell forward on his face. The body shook convulsively for a few minutes, the limbs moved about in a struggling way, then all was quiet."

The body measured five feet eight inches high.

Another day, when out hunting, M. du Chaillu heard a loud rumbling noise, which he took for thunder. Foreseeing a storm, he hastened to seek shelter under some ebony bushes, but he soon perceived that this supposed rolling of thunder was nothing else than the voice of a male gorilla calling the female, who an instant afterwards replied by a more feeble roar. The echo of this terrible voice resounded from mountain to mountain, and the forest seemed to tremble.

Our traveller immediately slipped a ball into his gun, already loaded with bird-shot, and walked in the direction of the cry.

From time to time the rumbling sound, which the male makes in striking his breast with his large fists, approached him.

He soon heard the cracking of branches, and he saw through the thicket a young tree rudely shaken, and in a few seconds fall to the ground. But perhaps the animal was conscious of danger, for a profound silence succeeded the roaring, and when M. du Chaillu had opened a passage into the thicket, the gorilla had disappeared.

"I am certain," writes he, "that I heard his roar at a distance of three miles, and the drumming of his arms against his breast at a mile at least. No words can describe the kind of thunder which it produces.

" On examining the wood where these gorillas were moving and feeding, I learnt for the first time why the canine teeth of this animal, especially of the male, are generally so worn, and I found at the same time astonishing proofs of his strength. Many trees, measuring from four to six inches in diameter, had been broken, and bore the marks of the biting of the gorillas, whose teeth had penetrated to the heart of the tree, in order to extract the pith. It was a hard wood, and I saw well, by the manner in which it had been gnawed, that

c

it was quite needless to attribute to any other cause the singular deterioration which I had remarked in the exterior of the canine teeth of these animals."

Some days after this fruitless encounter, the natives reported to Du Chaillu that a very-large gorilla had been seen many times in the forest ten miles to the east. The traveller, who was just then in search of such a subject for his collection, at once resolved to go and look after this fellow.

Accompanied by a negro named Gambo, he hunted for many hours, when at length, in a thicket at the bottom of an obscure ravine, he suddenly found himself face to face with two gorillas—male and female. These had already perceived them : the female uttered a cry of alarm and fled through the woods. As to the male, which was just the one which M. du Chaillu wanted, he showed no intention to fly. He rose slowly, and facing the disturbers of his retreat, he uttered a roar of rage. The hunters stood side by side awaiting the attack of the monster. Imperfectly seen in the dim half-light of the ravine, his hideous features working with rage, his eyes shining with a sombre fire, his satyr-like face violently contracted, he was altogether frightful.

He advanced by jerks, as is the custom of these animals, and halting from time to time to beat his fists on his vast breast, which emitted a dull hollow sound,

like that of a great bass drum covered with ox-hide;
then he gave a short bark, followed by that formidable
roar which we have already heard of.

The two men stood firm at their post for three long
minutes, waiting until the gigantic animal should be
sufficiently near. Arrived within a distance of about six
yards, the monster raised his head, roared again, and
beat his breast. He was on the point of moving forward again, when two balls, fired at the same moment,
staggered him, and he fell at full length on his face,
dead.

"I saw at once that we had the very animal I
wanted. It is the oldest of all my collection, and very
nearly the largest I ever saw. Gambo, who though a
young man was still an old hunter, said a few were
larger, but not many. Its height was five feet nine
inches, measured to the tip of the toes. Its arms
spread nine feet. Its chest had a circumference of
sixty-two inches. The hands—those terrible claw-like
weapons, with one blow of which he tears out the
bowels of a man, or breaks his arms—were of
immense muscular power, and bent like veritable claws.
I could see how frightful a blow could be struck with
such a hand, moved by such an arm, all swollen into
great bunches of muscular fibre, as this animal possessed. The big toe was no less than six inches in
circumference."

More Hunting Stories.

One morning, after a terrible night, during which an awful storm had extinguished the camp fire and left the travellers most uncomfortable, the roar of a gorilla was heard, which revived the drooping spirits of M. du Chaillu. He swallowed a cup of coffee and a biscuit— nothing more, for provisions were scarce—and set out.

"We had not far to go," he writes. "We had walked barely a quarter of a mile when we heard the loud roar again; this time quite near. We stood quite still for fear of alarming the beast, which was evidently approaching us, as we could see the bushes bent towards us. The fear of alarming him, however, proved needless. When he saw us he at once struck aside the intervening bushes, rose to an erect position, made a few steps, stopped, and seated himself; then, beating his vast breast, which resounded like an old drum, he advanced straight upon us. His dark eyes flashed with rage, his features worked convulsively, and at every few paces he stopped, and, opening his cavern- ous mouth, gave vent to his thunderous roar, which the forest gave back with multiplied echoes.

"He was evidently not a bit alarmed, and was quite ready for a fight. We stood perfectly still. He advanced till he stood beating his breast within six yards of us, when I thought it time to put an end to the scene.

My shot hit him in the breast, and he fell forward on his face, dead. They die very easily, and have none of that tenacity of life which most savage animals have. In this they also resemble man. It proved to be a middle-aged male, a fine specimen."

Still another encounter, and another victory. The animal had announced his presence by roaring. They thought he was close at hand, but he proved farther off than they imagined. They wandered nearly three-quarters of an hour through the forest before they reached him. As soon as he perceived the men he came resolutely towards them, uttering a succession of the short bark-like yells which denote his rage.

" His manner of approach gave me once more an opportunity to see with how much difficulty he supports himself in the erect posture. His short and slender legs are not able firmly to sustain the large body. They totter beneath the weight, and the walk is a sort of waddle, in which the long arms are used, in a clumsy way, to balance the body and keep up the ill-sustained equilibrium. Twice he sat down to roar, evidently not trusting himself to this exertion while standing.

" My gun was fresh loaded, and could be depended upon, so I stood in advance. I waited, as the negro rule is, till the huge beast was within six yards of me; then, as he once more stopped to roar, delivered my fire, and brought him down on his face, dead.

"It proved to be a male, full grown, but young. His huge canine tusks, his claw-like hands, the immense development of muscle on his arms and breast,—his whole appearance, in fact, proclaimed a giant strength. There is enough likeness to humanity in this beast to make a dead one an awful sight, even to accustomed eyes, as mine were by this time. I never quite felt that matter-of-course indifference, or that sensation of triumph which the hunter has when a good shot has brought him a head of his choice game. It was as though I had killed some monstrous creation, which yet had something of humanity in it. Well as I knew that this was an error, I could not help the feeling.

"This animal was five feet eight inches high. In the evening, Minsho brought in a young female he had shot, which measured three feet eight inches. All the hunts had not this happy issue. On one occasion, when M. du Chaillu was beating the woods at the head of a little troop, one of his bold companions had the imprudence to advance alone from the side where he expected to encounter a gorilla. For nearly an hour they had lost sight of him, when they heard a shot fired in the distance—then a second. They ran in the direction of the shot, hoping to find a dead gorilla, when suddenly the forest resounded with more terrible roars.

"Gambo seized my arms in great agitation, and we

hurried on, both filled with a dreadful and sickening alarm. We had not gone far when our worst fears were realized. The poor brave fellow who had gone off alone, was lying on the ground in a pool of his own blood, and I thought, at first, quite dead. His bowels were protruding through the lacerated abdomen. Beside him lay his gun, t'o stock was broken, and the barrel was bent and flattened. It bore plainly the marks of the gorilla's teeth.

"We picked him up, and I dressed his wounds as well as I could with rags torn from my clothes. When I had given him a little brandy to drink, he came to himself, and was able, but with great difficulty, to speak. He said that he had met the gorilla suddenly face to face, and that it had not attempted to escape. 'It was,' he said, 'a huge male, and seemed very savage.' It was in a very gloomy part of the wood, and the darkness, I suppose, made him miss. He said he took good aim, and fired when the beast was only about eight yards off. The ball merely wounded it in the side. It at once began beating its breast, and with the greatest rage advanced upon him.

"To run away was impossible. He would have been caught in the jungle before he had gone a dozen steps.

"He stood his ground, and as quickly as he could reloaded his gun. Just as he raised it to fire, the gorilla dashed it out of his hands, the gun going off in the fall; and then in an instant, and with a terrible roar, the animal gave him a tremendous blow with its immense paw, frightfully lacerating the abdomen, and with this single blow laying bare part of the intestines. As he sank bleeding to the ground, the monster seized the gun, and the poor hunter thought he would have his brains dashed out with it; but the gorilla seemed to have looked upon this also as an enemy, and in his rage almost flattened the barrel between his strong jaws.

"When we came upon the ground, the gorilla was gone. This is their mode when attacked—to strike one or two blows, and then leave the victims of their rage on the ground, and go off into the woods.

"We hunted up our companions and carried our poor fellow to the camp, where all was instantly excitement and sorrow. * * * He had to tell the whole story over again; and the people declared at once that this was no true gorilla that had attacked him, but a man—a wicked man turned into a gorilla. Such a being no man could escape, they said; and it could not be killed even by the bravest hunters."

He was killed, nevertheless, the following day; but his victim succumbed some hours afterwards.

" THE ANIMAL GAVE HIM A TREMENDOUS BLOW."   [*Page* 24.

IV.—Baby Gorillas.

M. du Chaillu, who had killed so many adult gorillas, had never taken one alive, and he thought it impossible that he ever should do so; but for the young it was a different matter, although the thing presented some difficulties.

Some hunters whom our traveller had taken into his service had gone out to beat the wood on his account. There were five of them, and as they were going noiselessly through the forest they heard the cry of a little gorilla calling his mother. It was about noon, and a profound silence reigned around. The cry was heard a second time, and the men, knowing what joy the capture of a young gorilla would cause their master, resolved to go over to the side from whence the sound proceeded. With their guns cocked they crept into the thicket, where they soon found certain signs that the mother was not far off; there was also the same ground for supposing that the male was in the neighbourhood; nevertheless, the brave fellows did not hesitate. In a dead silence, and scarce breathing, they crawled on. At a few yards in advance of them the bushes were shaken, and soon they perceived a young gorilla, seated on the ground eating some berries, and at a short distance sat his mother, occupied in the same way. Just as they were raising their guns to fire, she perceived them. The shots struck her, and she fell mortally wounded.

At the noise of the discharge, the little gorilla threw himself on his mother, clasped her with his arms, and hid himself in her bosom. But the triumphant cries of the hunters recalled him to himself, and he left the body of his mother, rushed up a tree, and scrambled nearly to the top, where he sat howling at them savagely.

The blacks were much embarrassed, being unwilling either to shoot him or to expose themselves to his bites. At last they agreed to cut down the tree; and profiting by the surprise of the little monster when he fell, they threw a sack over his head, which, however, did not prevent his giving one of them a fearful bite on the hand, and another had a piece taken out of his leg.

As this little beast, although very small, and the merest baby for age, was astonishingly strong, and as nothing would assuage his fury, they scarcely knew how to carry him. They finished by fixing his neck in a forked stick in such a way as to keep him at a safe distance, at the same time preventing his escape; and in this fashion they led him to M. du Chaillu. "I cannot," he writes, "describe the emotions which I felt. That single moment recompensed me for all the fatigue and suffering I had undergone in Africa."

The excitement in the village was intense. The

young gorilla roared and bellowed, and looked around wildly with his wicked little eyes, giving fair warning that if he could only get at some one he would take his revenge. In two hours they had built a strong bamboo house, with the bars sufficiently apart to enable the ape to see and to be seen. Here he was immediately deposited, and M. du Chaillu enjoyed the opportunity of tranquilly examining his prize.

"It was a young male, evidently not yet three years old. Its face and hands were very black; eyes not so much sunken as in the adult. The hair began just at the eyebrows and rose to the crown, where it was of a reddish-brown. It came down the sides of the face in lines to the lower jaw, much as our beards grow. The upper lip was covered with short coarse hair, the lower lip had longer hair. The eyelids very slight and thin; eyebrows straight, and three-quarters of an inch long.

"The whole back was covered with hair of an iron-grey, becoming dark nearer the arms, and quite white about the *anus;* chest and abdomen covered with hair, which was somewhat thin and short on the breast. On the arms the hair was longer than anywhere on the body, and of a greyish-black colour, caused by the roots of the hair being dark and the ends whitish. On the hands and wrists the hair was black, and came down to the second joints of the fingers, though one could see in the short down the beginning of the long black hair which lines the upper parts of the fingers in the adult. The hair of the legs was greyish-black, becoming blacker as it reached the ankles, the feet being covered with black hair.

"When I had the little fellow safely locked in his cage, I ventured a few encouraging words to him. He stood in the farthest corner, but as I approached, bellowed and made a precipitate rush at me, and though I retreated as quickly as I could, succeeded in catching my trousers, which he grasped with one of his feet and tore, retreating immediately to the corner farthest away. This taught me caution for the present, though I had hopes still of being able to tame him.

"He sat in his corner looking wickedly out of his grey eyes, and I never saw a more morose or more ill-tempered face than had this little beast.

"The first thing was, of course, to attend to the wants of my captive. I sent for some of the forest berries, which these animals are known to prefer, and placed these and a **cup** of water within his reach.

"He was exceedingly shy, and would neither eat nor drink till I had removed to a considerable distance.

"The second day found Joe, as I had named him, fiercer than the first. He rushed savagely at any one who stood even for a moment near his cage, and seemed ready to tear us all to pieces. I threw him to-day some pineapple leaves, of which I noticed he ate only the white parts.

" There seemed no difficulty about his food, though he refused now—and continued during his short life to refuse—all food, except such wild leaves and fruit as were gathered from his native woods for him.

" The third day he was still morose and savage, bellowing when any person approached, and either retiring to a distant corner or rushing to attack.

' " On the fourth day, while no one was near, the little rascal succeeded in forcing apart two of the bamboo rails which composed his cage, and made his escape. I came up just as his flight was discovered, and immediately got all the negroes together for pursuit, determining to surround the wood and recapture him. Running into my house to get one of my guns, I was startled by an angry growl issuing from under my low bedstead. It was Master Joe, who lay hid there, but anxiously watching my movements. I instantly shut the windows and called to my people to guard the door. When Joe saw the crowd of black faces, he became furious, and with his eyes glaring, and with every sign of rage in his little face and body, got out from beneath the bed. We shut the door at the same time, and left him master of the premises, preferring to devise some plan for his easy capture rather than to expose ourselves to his terrible teeth.

" Meantime Joe stood in the middle of the room, examining with some surprise the furniture. I watched with fear, lest the ticking of my clock should strike his ear, and perhaps lead to an assault upon that precious article.

" Finally, seeing him quite still, I despatched some fellows for a net, and opening the door quickly, threw this over his head; fortunately, we succeeded at the first throw in fatally entangling the young monster, who roared frightfully, and struck and kicked in every direction under the net. I took hold of the back of his neck, two men seized his arms, and another man his legs, and thus held by four men, this extraordinary little creature still proved most troublesome. We carried him as quickly as we could to the cage, which had been repaired, and there once more locked him in. I never saw so furious a beast in my life as he was; he darted at every one who came near, bit the bamboos of the house, glared at us with venomous and sullen eyes, and in every motion showed a temper thoroughly wicked and malicious; and as there was no change in this for two days thereafter, but continual moroseness, I tried what starvation would do towards breaking his spirit. It also began to be troublesome to procure his food from the woods, and I wanted him to become accustomed to civilized food, which was placed before him. But he would touch nothing of the kind; and as for temper, after starving him twenty-four hours, all I gained was that he came slowly up and took some berries from the forest out of my hand, immediately retreating to his corner to eat them.

"Daily attention from me for a fortnight more did not bring any further confidence from him than this. * * * At the end of this fortnight I came one day to feed him, and found that he had gnawed a bamboo to pieces slyly, and again made his escape. Luckily, he had but just gone. As I looked around I caught sight of Master Joey making off on all-fours, and with great speed, across the little prairie for a clump of trees.

"I called the men up, and we gave chase. * * * He did not ascend a tree, but stood defiantly at the border of the wood. About one hundred and fifty of us surrounded him. As we moved up he began to yell, and made a sudden dash at a poor fellow who was in advance, who, as he ran, tumbled down in a fright, and by his fall escaped, but also detained Joe sufficiently long for the nets to be brought to bear upon him.

"Four of us again bore him struggling into the village. This time I would not trust him to the cage, but had a little light chain fastened round his neck. This operation he resisted with all his might, and it took us quite an hour to securely chain the little fellow, whose strength was something marvellous.

* * * "To the last he continued utterly untame-

able ; and, after his chains were on, added the vice of treachery to his others.

"He would come sometimes quite readily to eat out of my hand, but while I stood by him would suddenly— looking me all the time in the face, to keep my attention—put out his foot and grasp my leg. Several times he tore my pantaloons in this manner, quick retreat on my part saving my person, till at last I was obliged to be very careful in my approaches.

"The negroes could not come near him at all without setting him in a rage.

"After he was chained, I filled a half-barrel with hay, and set it near him for his bed. He recognized its use at once, and it was pretty to see him shake up the hay and creep into this nest when he was tired. At night he always again shook it up, and then took some hay in his hands, with which he would cover himself when he was snug in his barrel. Ten days after he was thus chained he died suddenly. He was in good health, and ate plentifully of his natural food, which was brought every day for him. He did not seem to sicken until two days before his death, and died in some pain."

Some months later he was replaced by another one. This time M. du Chaillu took part in the capture of the young animal.

"We were walking along in silence, when I heard a cry, and presently saw before me a female gorilla, with a tiny baby gorilla hanging at her breast and sucking. The mother was stroking the little one, and looking fondly down at it; and the scene was so pretty and touching, that I held my fire, and considered, like a soft-hearted fellow, whether I had not better leave them in peace.

"Before I could make up my mind, however, my hunter fired, and killed the mother, who fell without a struggle. The mother fell, but the baby clung to her, and with pitiful cries endeavoured to attract her attention. I came up, and when it saw me it hid its poor little head in its mother's breast; it could neither walk nor bite, so we could easily manage it, and I carried it while the men bore the mother on a pole. When we got to the village, another scene ensued. The men put the body down, and I set the little fellow near. As soon as he saw his mother, he crawled to her and threw himself on her breast. He did not find his accustomed nourishment, and I saw that he perceived something was the matter with the old one. He crawled over her body, smelt at it, and gave utterance from time to time to a plaintive cry, 'hoo, hoo, hoo!' which touched my heart.

"I could get no milk for the poor little fellow, who could not eat, and consequently died on the third day after he was caught. He seemed more docile than the other I had, for he already recognized my voice, and would try to hurry towards me when he saw me."

A third time M. du Chaillu succeeded in procuring a young living gorilla, under the following circumstances :—

He had been hunting for about an hour, when the cry of a young gorilla calling to his mother was heard. Two men, who were in advance, and who were well accustomed to life in the woods, knelt down and crawled through the bushes; about half an hour afterwards two shots were heard. M. du Chaillu ran and found the mother shot dead, but the young one had saved itself in the woods.

They concealed themselves in order to wait for its return. They had not to wait long,—it reappeared, jumped on its mother, and began to suck and to caress her. The hunters rushed upon it immediately, but although the little animal was evidently less than two years old, it fought with so much force that it succeeded in escaping.

It was retaken, nevertheless; not, however, until one of the men had been severely bitten in the arm by the little demon. It was a female. When brought back to its mother, it threw itself upon her, and buried its head in the maternal bosom. It was a touching sight. Unhappily, this little female only lived ten days; she was not as ferocious as the young male already described, but she was quite as cunning. When she was approached, she exhibited the same menacing demonstrations. Her eyes, though milder, had the same false and traitorous look, " and," writes M. du Chaillu, " she had the same way as my other intractable captive, of looking you straight in the eyes when she was meditating an attack. I remarked, also, the same manœuvre practised by the other when she wanted to seize anything—say my arm, which, by reason of her chain, she could not reach with her arm ; she looked me straight in the face, then, quick as a flash, threw her body on one leg and arm, and reached out with the other leg. Several times I had narrow escapes of a grip from her strong great toe. * * * All her motions were remarkably quick, and her strength, though she was so small and young, was truly extraordinary."

CHAPTER II.

Bears.

I.—GRIZZLY BEARS.

OF all the quadrupeds of America, the grizzly bear is
the only one that is truly formidable, and therefore his
manners, his habits, and his exploits are the favourite
theme of the hunters of the West. His size is enormous, and his strength prodigious ; his speed far
superior to that of a man endeavouring to escape from
him by flight. His claws are nearly nine inches in
length. Although he is very fond of fruits, acorns, and
roots, he is carnivorous as well as herbivorous. He
attacks the buffalo, fells him to the ground, and drags
him to some spot where he can feed on him at leisure.

If a man attacks him, he squats on his hind paws
and accepts the combat ; and when pressed by hunger,
he becomes the assailant. When wounded, he becomes
furious, and then the tables are turned, and man is
hunted. He was formerly known on the Missouri and
in the low countries, but, like the tribes of the prairies,
he has gradually beaten retreat before the march of civi-

HUNTERS PURSUED BY A BEAR.

[Page 36.

lization, and to-day he is only to be found in elevated regions,—in the Rocky Mountains, for example, and in the Black Mountains, a great chain situated about thirty-three leagues to the east of them. There he hides himself in caverns, or in holes scooped out by himself under the roots and trunks of fallen trees.

Hunters, whether red or white, regard the hunting of the bear as the most heroic of all the field sports on the American continent. They prefer attacking him on horseback, and sometimes they approach sufficiently near to touch him, but woe to the horse or the rider that gets too near to his terrible claws! The man must have a sure eye and a steady hand to strike the animal in a vital part, for he is very difficult to kill; and it very rarely happens that one shot kills him, unless it passes through his head or his heart.

Some Americans on a commercial expedition had one evening established their camp at the foot of the Black Mountains. Soon, from the numerous footprints among the bushes, they discovered that their tents were pitched just in the very midst of one of the rendezvous of grizzly bears. From that moment all the charm of the encampment was destroyed.

The night, however, was passed very well, but they had sufficient proof next morning that their fears had not been groundless.

"Amongst the hired men of the party was one

William Cannon, who had been a soldier at one of the frontier posts.

" He was an inexperienced hunter and a poor shot, for which he was much bantered by his more adroit comrades. Piqued at their raillery, he had been practising ever since he joined the expedition, but without success. One afternoon he went out alone, and, to his great joy, he had the good fortune to kill a buffalo. Being at a considerable distance from the camp, he cut out the tongue and some of the choice bits, made a packet of them, and slinging it on his shoulders by a strap passed round his forehead, as travellers carry packets of merchandise, he directed his steps all glorious for the camp.

" In passing through a narrow ravine he heard footsteps behind him. He looked round, and saw to his great terror that he was followed by a grizzly bear, apparently attracted by the smell of the meat. Cannon had heard so much of the invulnerability of this tremendous animal, that he not only did not attempt to fire at him, but, slipping the strap from his forehead, let go the buffalo-meat and ran for his life. The bear, without stopping for the game, pursued the hunter. He had nearly overtaken him, when Cannon reached a tree, and scrambled up it, throwing down his rifle.

" An instant after, bruin was at the foot of the tree; but as this kind of bear does not climb, he contented himself by changing his pursuit into a blockade. Night came on. Poor Cannon could not know for certain in the darkness whether his enemy remained there or not, but his fears pictured him rigorously mounting guard, and he passed the night in the tree, a prey to the most horrible fancies. At daybreak the bear was gone. Cannon warily descended, picked up his gun, and made the best of his way back to the camp, without troubling himself to go in search of the buffalo-meat."

John Day, an old Kentucky hunter, accompanied by one of the clerks, a lively youngster, was following the trail of a deer, when suddenly a huge grizzly bear emerged from the thicket at thirty yards distant, rearing himself on his hind-legs with a terrific growl, and displaying a hideous array of claws and teeth. The young man instantly levelled his gun, but John Day's iron hand was quickly upon his arm. " Be quiet, boy, be quiet ! " said the hunter between his clenched teeth, without turning his eyes from the bear.

The two hunters remained motionless. The monster regarded them for several minutes, then dropping his fore-feet, slowly withdrew.

After a few steps he turned round, sat up again, and repeated his menaces. Day's hand was still on the arm of his young companion, whilst he repeated between his teeth, " Quiet boy ! keep quiet, keep quiet ! " a warning but little needed, for the young man had not moved.

At length the bear again came down on all-fours, retreated another twenty yards, then turned round, showed his teeth, and growled. This third menace was too much for the game spirit of John Day.

"By Jove!" exclaimed he, "I can stand this no longer;" and in an instant a ball from his rifle whizzed into the foe. The wound was not mortal, but luckily it dismayed instead of enraging the animal, and he retreated into the thicket.

Day's young companion reproached him for not practising the caution which he preached.

"Look here, my boy," replied the veteran, "caution is caution; but one must not put up with too much, even from a bear. Would you have me suffer myself to be bullied all day by a varmint?" *

"A hunter, whilst pursuing a deer, fell into one of those deep funnel-shaped pits, formed on the prairies by the settling of the waters after heavy rains, and known by the name of sink-holes.

"To his great horror he found himself in contact, at the bottom of the pit, with a huge grizzly bear. The monster grappled him, a deadly contest ensued,

---

* Washington Irving's "Astoria."

and the poor hunter was severely torn and bitten, and had an arm and a leg broken, but succeeded in killing his rugged foe.

"For several days he remained at the bottom of the pit, too much crippled to move, and subsisting on the raw flesh of the bear. At length he regained sufficient strength to scramble to the top of the pit, and crawling into a ravine formed by a nearly dry watercourse, he took a delicious draught. The fresh water infused new life into him. Then dragging himself along from pool to pool, he sustained himself with small fish and frogs.

"One day he saw a wolf kill a deer in the neighbouring prairie; he instantly scrambled out of the ravine, scared away the wolf, and, lying down beside the carcase of the deer, he remained there until he had made several hearty meals, by which his strength was much recruited.

"Returning to the ravine, he followed the watercourse to a point where it grew to be a considerable stream. He descended this river, allowing himself to be guided by the current, and just at the point where it emptied into the Mississippi, he found a fallen tree, which he launched with some difficulty, and getting astride of it, committed himself to the current of the mighty river. In this way he floated along until he arrived opposite the Fort at Council Bluffs.

" Happily, he arrived by daylight, otherwise he might have passed this solitary post unperceived, and have perished in the idle waste of waters. Being descried from the Fort, a canoe was sent to his relief, and he was brought to shore more dead than alive, where he soon recovered of his wounds, but remained maimed for life."*

II.—The Brown Bear.

The manner in which the Russian peasants hunt this bear is worthy of description. The weapon of the Fins is a lance. At about a foot from the point a bar of iron is fixed crosswise, the object being to prevent the lance from penetrating too deeply into the body of the animal, and causing him, pierced through and through, to fall upon the hunter.

When this latter has discovered the bear's winter quarters, he posts himself, with his dog, near the entrance. The dog barks, the man shouts, and both making the greatest noise possible, endeavour to irritate the solitary animal and bring him out of his den.

For a long time the bear hesitates, but at last,

---

* Irving's "Journey in the Prairies."

"THE FIN WALKS STRAIGHT UP TO THE ENCOUNTER."

[Page 48.

tired of these provocations, he rushes* out in great fury.

At sight of the peasant he rises on his hams and springs forth; but the Fin is ready for him, holding in front the iron point of his lance pressed against his breast, and carefully concealing the stem, in order that the length of the weapon may not arouse the suspicion of the animal, who otherwise would parry with his paws the blow which the hunter is ready to give him. The latter walks straight up to the encounter, and, when the distance between them is so little that the monster, extending his arms, is on the point of reaching him, suddenly the weapon is darted forth, with a firm hand and a sure eye, through the heart of the bear.

Had the bar of iron not been placed thus crosswise, the animal, although mortally wounded, would have fallen on the man and have done him serious injury, but this bar arrests him in his spring, and the hunter soon turns him over. "What will seem extraordinary," says a naturalist, "is that the bear, instead of endeavouring to tear out the lance, holds it tightly with his paws, and forces it more deeply into the wound."

This triumph is concluded by a little *fête*, at which there is always present a poet to sing the valour of the hunter.

The wearing of bearskins, like that of furs, is not always free from inconvenience, and I shall not wander from my subject in citing, as *à propos*, an episode from the "Voyage d'Acerbi."

He was crossing in a sledge the Gulf of Finland, which was entirely frozen over.

"I expected," he writes, "to have to cross a limitless' and monotonous plain. What was my astonishment, my admiration—even my fright, the farther we got from our point of departure! Enormous masses of ice, heaped up one above another, sometimes in the form of rocks, sometimes of pointed pyramids! What *détours* we had to make, in order to avoid these groups of ice which barred our way! In spite of all precautions, our sledges upset one after the other, and constantly brought the caravan to a stand. One circumstance, impossible to foresee, increased the dangers which surrounded us. The sight of our long pelisses, made of Russian wolf or bearskins, and the odour which they exhaled, frightened some of our horses, and made them furious. When it became necessary to disengage ourselves from our upset sledges, the horses perceived us, and taking us for the animals with whose skins we were covered, would plunge in their harness, or start off at full gallop. The peasant, fearing to lose his horse, would cling to the bridle, and rather than let go, would allow himself, at the risk of his life, to be dragged over the rough ice until his horse was stopped.

" Then we would regain our sleighs, and the conductor, taught by experience, would take the precaution to bandage the eyes of his horses. One of these animals, nevertheless, the fiercest and most spirited in our caravan, took fright, and managed to escape altogether. The peasant who was driving him, after being dragged over the ice for a long time, at last let go the bridle, and then the horse, free from all restraint, redoubled his speed and broke through all obstacles; the sledge which he was carrying away, bounding over the ice, added to his fright and lent wings to his speed. We followed him for a long time with our eyes, until at length he was lost in the horizon. We saw him again and again, as he surmounted the frozen waves, like a black speck, gradually diminishing, till at last he totally disappeared. His master took a reserve sledge, and started off in pursuit, flattering himself that he should find him by following in his track. For ourselves, we continued our route towards the Isle of Aland, taking, as well as we could, the middle of the smoothest passages, not, however, without being frequently upset, and in danger of losing one or other of our horses, which would have caused us no small embarrassment."

III.—The White Bear.

The white bear enjoys a reputation for ferocity which does not yield to that of the grizzly, and his character will not be changed for the better by what we are about to tell of him.

A ship returning from Nova Zembla having cast anchor off one of the islands at the mouth of the Strait of Waigatz, two sailors had the curiosity to visit that island.

After walking about there for some time, they sat down on the shore, in sight of the vessel.

They were chatting tranquilly together when one of them suddenly felt himself seized forcibly by the back of the neck.

He at first supposed it to be one of those rough jokes in which sailors sometimes indulge. "Who is squeezing me so?" cried he.

The other sailor, turning round, uttered a cry of alarm—"Oh, my God, it is a bear!" and he ran away.

It was, in fact, an enormous but very lean white bear, which had stealthily approached the two mariners, and which soon made a corpse of the one who had fallen into his clutches.

Aroused by the desperate cries of the other, the ship's crew, armed with pikes and guns, threw themselves into the boats, landed on the island, and went straight to the bear gloating on his prey.

The bear saw them approach without moving and without discontinuing his repast; and when they had approached near him, he started up, and rushing upon them, seized one by the middle of his body, and throwing him down, dragged him away in sight of his stupefied companions, and tore him to pieces with his teeth!

At this sight a panic arose amongst the sailors, and they ran away much faster than they came, threw themselves into their boats, and, full of terror, scrambled into the vessel.

Once in safety, courage returned to them; and feeling ashamed of themselves, and intensely excited, the proposition was made to return in a body to land, and attack the ferocious animal, wherever they might encounter him.

Notwithstanding, some of them protested; and their sage discourse is worthy of being transcribed as the historian gives it:—

" Our comrades are dead," said they; " we cannot bring them to life again; there is no longer any hope of saving them. We shall not go to encounter their murderer, but to see their limbs scattered hither and thither, and to renew our grief at sight of their broken bones and torn flesh. What honour can there be in running after an inglorious victory, which must be bought at the price of a thousand dangers?"

How many were there whom this eloquence did not touch?—Three! They started at the same instant, trusting to nothing but their courage, and very sure of having no assistance.

Crouching over the two bodies, the conqueror was about to profit by his victory. They advanced, and, apparently at too great a distance, they fired several times without touching him. Then the bravest man of the three, separating from the others, approached nearer, and taking good aim, he hit the bear a little above the eye, the ball passing through his head.

The bear did not fall; he did not even leave his prey. Far from that, he arose, and holding the body by the neck, fled away. He had only gone a few steps, however, when they saw him stagger, and the sailors attacked him with their sabres.

The terrible beast fell at length, but he did not leave hold of his man until they had plunged a sword into his mouth, and given him the *coup de grâce*.

Then the brave fellows gathered the remains of their comrades, and buried them on the island, in presence of the whole crew, who could now land without the fear of breaking the rules of prudence.

The skin of the bear was awarded to the man

"HE HIT THE BEAR A LITTLE ABOVE THE EYE." [Page 48.

who first struck him; it measured thirteen feet in length.

Here is another story to show that the white bear dies a hard death :—

We are on board the ship of Captain Jonge Kees. It is evening. They had been cutting up a large quantity of whale blubber during the evening. The captain and crew, overcome by fatigue, had retired to rest. No one remained on deck but the ordinary watch. The ship was made fast to a bank of ice. On that bank the men on duty saw a bear lying down, and apparently asleep.

"Let us go and surprise him," said they; and off they went, as quietly as possible, in order not to awake any one. But they could not avoid making some noise in detaching the boat. The captain, who only slept with one ear, heard them: he had just been dreaming of a whale, and thinking they had discovered one, he arose, went on deck, and learning what was the matter, and having verified the fact with his telescope, and judging that one boat would not suffice, he armed another, and started off with his men.

The bear saw this little army approaching without at first showing any disquietude; but when the boats were close upon the bank, without waiting longer, he quitted his place and plunged into the water.

They followed him with the utmost speed, and soon

gaining on him, the captain had the honour of striking the first blow with the spear, which pierced his entrails.

They might have redoubled their blows, but as it was his skin they most wanted, and they were fearful of damaging it, they resolved to give him time to die of that first wound, which could not be long.

Nevertheless, the animal continued to swim, reached a little island which arose only about five feet above the water, and began to climb up, to the astonishment of the sailors, who could not believe him capable of making such an effort; he squatted himself down there, with his muzzle on his fore-paws.

Then the captain became impatient. He steered on to the island, landed, and with a long lance he prepared to strike a second blow. The bear, which he thought was nearly dead, roared, and making a gigantic bound, fell on him, and placing one paw on his side and the other on his breast, showed him two rows of white teeth.

He remained in that position, which a painter would have paid dear to see, looking at the man as if he desired (says the report from which we quote) to give him time to consider all the horror of the punishment, and to lengthen out his cruel vengeance.

The crew (continues the report) no sooner saw the imminent danger of their chief, than they shouted with all their might towards the ship for more help. But a sailor, who did not expect that the bear would have the complaisance to await the arrival of assistance, scrambled on to the island, and, armed with a boat-hook, ran to the defence of the captain, and attacked the bear. The boat-hook was a weapon very badly chosen. Happily, at sight of this new adversary, the animal took flight. The captain had not even a scratch.

A reinforcement arrived from the ship, and they took counsel together.

The bear had not gone far, and was sitting on an ice-bank. They attacked him at first with their guns, and then with spears, until at length he succumbed, but not until the whole crew had joined in the attack.

CHAPTER III.

The Tiger.

"Sitting by the camp fire in the forests of the Don, I have sometimes heard a deep low moan, like the rumbling of falling earth. The native servants would exchange glances of intelligence, and, affrighted, would cease their gossip on the price of corn; and then the conversation would soon turn on the innumerable cases of death or of wounds caused by the fiercest and most subtle enemy that the sportsman can encounter in India."

Thus Captain Dunlop, of the Indian army, expresses himself at the end of his recitals of the chase in the Himalayas.*

It is by this plaintive sigh that the royal tiger makes known his presence to the hosts of the forest. In company with other animals of his species, he caterwauls like a gigantic Tom-cat. His springs, when charging, are accompanied by a series of rapid frightful, cough-like growls; "But," says the Captain, "I have heard

---

* "Hunting in the Himalayas."

a bear making nearly the same noise;" and M. Louis Viardot says the same.*

With one blow of his paw he will break the back of an ox, and will carry him afterwards as a cat carries a mouse, and apparently without effort; and it rarely happens that the limbs of the victim touch the ground.

II.

MOUNTED on elephants, some Europeans, among whom were some indigo planters and officers of a native regiment, left Bombay, intending to devote some time to the noble pleasure of tiger hunting. They had not yet reached the skirt of the forest, when the noise of their march aroused a huge tigress, which, far from flying, attacked furiously the line of elephants. One of these animals, seeing the tiger for the first time, was frightened, and in spite of the efforts of the hunter who rode him, turned tail on the terrible beast. Seeing this, the tigress rushed in pursuit, leaped on the elephant's back, seized the hunter by the thigh, dragged him to the ground, and, throwing him over her shoulders

---

* "The bear advanced resolutely, in a straight line, the head raised, and uttered at intervals a blusterous hissing, like that which a cat makes when barked at by a dog."--*Souvenirs de Chasse*, p. 791.

as easily as a fox would have thrown a fowl, bounded off towards the forest. All the guns were at once directed towards her, but no hunter dared to fire, in the fear of hitting their unfortunate companion.

They were soon out of sight, but they could follow by the trace of blood shed by the victim. Soon these traces became more and more indistinct, and, arrived in the heart of the forest, not knowing on which side to direct their steps, the hunters, in despair, were about to give up the pursuit, when at the very moment they least expected it, they perceived the tigress and her prey, both extended in the high grass. The beast was dead. The man, with his eyes wide open, was still conscious, but his thigh remained in the jaws of the tigress, and he was too feeble to reply to the questions of his friends. It was necessary, in order to release him from his terrible position, to cut off the head of the animal, and to disjoint her jaws.

Fortunately, a surgeon was present, and the best care was given to the wounded, and he was conveyed to the nearest dwelling from the theatre of this frightful scene.

When he had sufficiently regained his strength, he related his adventure thus:—Stunned by his fall, weakened by loss of blood and by pain, he had fainted a few seconds after the tigress seized him. When he regained consciousness he found himself on the back of the animal, which was trotting at a rapid pace towards the thicket. Every second his face and his hands were torn by the bushes through which the tigress carried him. His death appeared to him certain, and he remained motionless, resigned to his fate. Then the thought struck him that he had in his belt a pair of pistols. He seized one of them, and pointing it at the animal's head, he fired. The tigress shook violently, her teeth were pressed more deeply into the flesh of her victim, and that was all. The poor fellow fainted again. When he came to himself once more, wishing to try his last chance, he took his second pistol, and this time aimed under the shoulder-blade, in the direction of the heart, and the tigress fell dead, without a struggle or a groan, whilst the hunter, exhausted by this last effort, had not even strength to shout to his friends when he heard them approach.

III.

LET us return to Captain Dunlop.

He started one morning from the camp of Jubrawalla, on the banks of the Sooswa, accompanied by Major R——. They had with them seven elephants. Near this spot was a piece of land covered with young cotton plants and thick boxwood bushes. As the hunters were crossing this ground, they perceived the carcase of an ox, partly devoured by some animal, which to all appearances had only just quitted his feast. The ground was too hard to judge of the animal from the footprints. Nevertheless, they immediately formed in line, and the hunt commenced along a dry trench, partly covered by the jungle. At the first turn of the route an animal sprang out of the ditch, and for a second stood on the opposite bank, at a distance of sixty yards from the hunters. A ghoorka declared that it was a calf; but it proved to be a full-grown tigress.

Pursuit commenced immediately. The animal rushed across a large piece of ground, on which the grass had been burnt, but the most that it could do, being gorged with food, was to keep just in advance of the line of the seven elephants, which were rushing forward at their utmost speed.

The tigress charged straight through a herd of cattle, which immediately dispersed. At length, after a race of about two miles, she reached a part of the jungle which crossed a deep *nullah*, and the hunt began again. "Scarcely had I entered that part of the jungle which I was about to search, when I saw her under a bush, crouching down, ready to make a spring; and firing one barrel straight between her eyes, she rolled over into the *nullah*. She threw herself repeatedly against the side in her attempts to remount, but failed to accomplish it, all troubled as she was

"R—— DESPATCHED HER WITH A BALL BEHIND THE EAR."

[*Page* 51.

from the effects of my ball, which had made a large fracture in her skull, grazed the brain, and caused an overflowing of blood in the throat. The shot was fatal, for it was impossible for her to leave the place; and R——, who came up soon afterwards, despatched her with a ball behind the ear."

The carcase was hoisted on one of the elephants; not, however, without the latter protesting by sundry imprecations and objections after his fashion.

Another time (it was in 1855, at the famous fair of Hurdwar) two or three millions of people, from all parts of India,—Thibet, the Punjaub, Affghanistan, and Persia, were assembled at this religious and commercial rendezvous; and Captain Dunlop was present as superintendent of the mountain district.

The second day a native came to tell him that in the very midst of that immense assembly a tiger had just struck down a man. The Captain immediately distributed rifles amongst some officers who were on a visit near him, and they started off, to the number of seven. Unfortunately, there was no hunting elephant in the camp, and they were obliged to content themselves with three saddle elephants, although it was almost certain that they would turn tail at the critical moment. Each elephant carried two hunters, and the seventh, Mr. O. Bradford, rode on horseback.

At the distance of about 500 yards they found the

unfortunate countryman, with his skull fractured and his brains uncovered. A little farther on they were shown, in the midst of a field of wheat, a thicket about thirty yards square. It was from this thicket that the tiger had thrown himself upon his victim, and there also he had taken refuge.

Some thousands of the natives, seeing the hunters, united together around the place, enclosing the tiger in a living circle. It was fortunate for Mr. Dunlop and his friends that they were mounted on the elephants, for on foot it would have been impossible to discharge their guns without wounding some one in the crowd. Now let the narrator speak:—

"Our feline friend, evidently arrived at a pitch of lively excitement, did not await our arrival, but charged upon us of his own accord with a cry of rage.

"The three elephants with one accord faced about, and ran one against the other, screaming and crying with fright, whilst Bradford danced around them on my chestnut, 'Waverley.' Several shots were nevertheless fired by our quadrille, and with some success, inasmuch as whilst neither of us was hit, one ball was sent through the fore-leg of the tiger just in time to stop short his charge, and to send him back into the cover.

"An active struggle now began between the elephants and their drivers, seeing that no force, moral or physical, no caressing or spurring, could induce them to form in line, to beat the thicket out of which had come the monster which had so troubled their minds.

"At last, pell-mell, and driven like sheep, they advanced to about fifty yards from the thicket, guided only by the violent blows of the *ankus*, when a second roar from the tiger served as a prelude to a fresh charge with all his speed.

" This would doubtless have been, from the manner in which it was made, a flight to his lair, but luckily, amongst the numerous shots fired from the howdahs, which were rolling and pitching like boats on the sea, a ball, fired by Melville, struck the tiger's shoulder, which sent him rolling at four feet from Grant's elephant, where we saw him lying on his back, with his hind-legs paralyzed, and performing the exercise of a pugilist with his fore-legs. The roars of the elephants, the howling of the tiger, and the cries of the crowd, produced such a confusion, that Melville's elephant faced completely round and took to his heels.

" The hurrah which followed the fall of the tiger had scarcely subsided when he arose, and, balancing himself, attempted to spring forward a few yards, principally by means of his fore-paws. He repeated this manœuvre at each discharge : it seemed as if each ball had a revivifying effect on his system, like sal volatile. He had risen for the last time, when some of us descended from our elephants to examine him more closely.

"He was found to be a male, and one of the largest I had ever seen:"

IV.

Another hunter, and similar stories. Our guide is now M. Thomas Anquetil. The scene is in Birmah, at some miles from Ngnyoun-gôo, in a forest, in the centre of which a lake occupies the place of an ancient monastery which had been destroyed by an earthquake. This lake is covered by water-fowl.

Accompanied by a European, M. le Baron de L——, his servants, and a few natives, amongst whom was one named Laos, M. Thomas Anquetil went out hunting.

Going along by the side of the lake on foot, the narrator separated from his companions, and followed only by an Indian rower, who had charge of his rifle, had just fired both barrels on a flight of birds. The Indian went forward immediately to gather up the dead and the wounded. "He had not gone twenty yards when a sharp, piercing, and terrible roar resounded through the solitudes of the forest, and was re-echoed by the neighbouring rocks. Soon I heard a rapid movement, and then a tiger sprang from the

"HE COULD NOT FIRE, FOR THE MAN AND THE TIGER WERE SO ENTANGLED."

[Page 61

bushes, which he broke like straw. The tiger was forty yards off. The Indian stood still, aimed, and fired; a fresh roar, and the ferocious beast pursued his course.

"At twenty yards the Indian fired his second barrel; a frightful cry of terror and agony was the reply. The tiger at one bound reached and seized his enemy, and tore him in pieces!"

M. Thomas Anquetil threw down his rifle, and taking his revolver in his right hand and his cutlass in his left, he held himself in readiness; he could not fire, for the man and the tiger were so entangled together. At length the animal, with his eyes on fire, his mouth all bloody, and lashing his sides with his tail, abandoned the dead body, and turning round upon the hunter, prepared for a spring, when six shots resounded. All the balls had struck, and the animal rolled on the ground, uttering a convulsive groan.

"The Indian was reduced to a shapeless heap. He had not left his hold on my rifle. His cramped fingers still clung with one hand to the stock and the other to the barrel of the gun. The wood was broken and the barrels bore marks of the tiger's fangs.

"The ferocious beast—it was a female—lay on the left side, the claws stiffened, the pupils contracted, the mouth dripping with blood, slimy foam, and shreds of throbbing flesh. She belonged to the species called the Royal Tiger, which I recognized by the short nap, strewn with black and irregular rays over the tawny hair. But its height and length, the fineness of its extremities, and the grace of its form, denoted that it was not yet quite full grown. I suppose it was about seven years old.

"The oarsman's ball had glided over the ribs and ploughed the right flank of the beast; the second had entered the flesh at the top of the shoulder. One inch lower, and the Indian would have conquered the tiger, for he would have broken the joint. He had evidently fired each time a little too hastily.

"Two of my six balls had shattered the tiger's jaw; the four others were lodged in the breast, and one of them had grazed the heart.

"Scarcely had our inspection terminated when Laos, who had carefully watched all, pressed under his finger the slightly distended udder of the beast, and there issued a yellowish-white milky fluid. This was a ray of sunlight to him. He seized his cutlass and started off, without speaking a word, and began to search about the end of the peninsula, beating every tuft of bushes. The Baron and I, being greatly moved, took up our firearms and set ourselves to watch with increasing interest.

"At the end of the peninsula footprints were seen on the greasy and humid shore—some large and deep, others small and almost imperceptible. Laos at once guessed the meaning. The beasts had come there to quench their thirst, after which they had gone away on different tracks.

"At one place, where the grass and the shrubs had been more trodden down than elsewhere, as if many beasts had made their halt there, Laos remarked that the track in front, which was that of the mother, was much more decided than the light impression which was seen on the left. This last index was sufficient. At forty yards farther a shout escaped from him.

"Under a covering of lotus and flowering rushes, two young tigers, a little larger than cats, as round as balls, lay one against the other, awaiting their mother in a kind of fierce terror. They were about three weeks or a month old at most. Laos having half opened with the point of his stick this verdant screen, they opened their eyes, stretched out their claws, showed their teeth, and growled: with one blow with the butt-end of his gun he stunned them both.

"To tie their legs together with cords, to take off his vest, and to divest himself of his *patsóo* (he was then naked as a glass, about which he did not trouble himself the least in the world), was for him an affair of half a minute.

"Then he extended his vest on the ground, and placed thereon the two little animals, and tied up the opposite ends.   Then having opened out his *patsóo*, he enclosed the packet, and placing it on a branch over his shoulder, he marched away, after the fashion of a country labourer.

"The hunters returned through the forest, M. Thomas Anquetil and the Baron walking ahead, in conversation.

"Suddenly a warm breath passed over my cheek; I felt myself seized by my girdle from behind, and the grave voice of Laos murmured rapidly these words in my ear,—'Take care, master; do not advance.'

"'What is it, then?'

"'A tiger!' said he, extending his arm.

"This dialogue took place whilst I was taking down my rifle, which was unfortunately fixed in my shoulder-belt.

"A little eminence of twelve or fifteen feet overhung the route.   Around a mango tree of moderate growth was a cluster of flowering mallows.

"The tiger, the position of whose body we could guess at, but as yet we could only see his head, was watching us with a fixed gaze, his back against the tree, and his body bent under him, in order to give double force to his spring.   He was waiting until we should arrive in front of him, to throw himself upon us suddenly and at one bound; the interval which separated us was scarcely thirty yards.

"When we stood to take aim at him he understood that he was discovered. A slight movement on one side, as if to examine where he could fly, betrayed this instinctive sentiment. Then all at once, obeying his sanguinary nature, or rather his courage, he turned to us suddenly, and crouching on his haunches, prepared to spring on us.

"Immediately I called out, 'One! two! three!—fire!'

"He fell on the path like a lump of lead, at five or six yards from the foot of the eminence, so great was the impulse of the fall; and, strange to say, without a cry or a groan.

"He remained there—his fore-legs extended; his hind legs hidden underneath him; his nose buried in the dust: one might have said that he was asleep. But was he really dead, or only stunned?

"We advanced whilst loading our guns; and, in the meantime, my people kept their eyes on him. Not seeing him move, I had a great desire to riddle his head with the balls of my revolver, remaining at a few yards' distance; for the tiger, like the lion, has sometimes sudden starts and returns of fury, which are extremely dangerous. Let him reach you at such a moment, and you are lost. His paw fells you, his claws rip you open, and his teeth crush your limbs, were he at the very point of expiring.

"Laos dissuaded me, saying that I should injure the

F

skin, and he begged of me to let him do it. I consented; but, nevertheless, I continued to aim at the animal, at all hazards.

" Laos deposited his burden of the two young tigers on the ground, and then, taking up his club with his two hands by the extremity of the handle, he placed himself well in front of the beast, and dealt him a blow on the head with all his might, with so much vigour, indeed, as to split the skull in two as a butcher would that of an ox.

" It was a full-grown male; and a very splendid animal he was.

" Laos took the fancy to draw the scent of the beast before the two cubs, still wrapped up in the *patsoo;* they squalled and tore like mad things, until they very nearly managed to effect their escape. This was evidence to me that the tiger was their father.

" Poor Laos ended very badly. M. Thomas-Anquetil had made him a present of a rifle and ammunition, of which no one could make better use. One day, surprised by a tiger, he promptly put himself on the defensive. His two barrels missed fire in the very face of the animal, and he was devoured in the twinkling of an eye."

THE LION OF SOUTH AFRICA.　　[*Page* 67.

CHAPTER IV.

The Lion of South Africa.

THE lion of South Africa, or the *dog-nosed* lion, differs considerably from the lion of Northern Africa in its physical characteristics and its habits, as well as in its size, strength, and courage; and the following anecdotes will serve to exhibit some of these characteristics.

"When," says Livingstone, "a lion is met in the daytime, a circumstance by no means infrequent to travellers in these parts, if preconceived notions do not lead them to expect something very 'noble' or 'majestic,' they will see merely an animal, somewhat larger than the biggest dog they ever saw, and partaking very strongly of the canine features. The face is not much like the usual drawings of a lion, the nose being prolonged like a dog's; not exactly such as our painters make it, though they might learn better at the Zoological Gardens: their ideas of majesty being usually shown by making their lions' faces like old women in nightcaps."

It should, however, be said in reply to this, in the first place, that hitherto painters have never had South African lions for their models ; and then that this lion, although less formidable than the lion of the Atlas, is, nevertheless, not quite so contemptible an animal as the worthy traveller would have us believe.

II.

One of the characteristic traits of this or that variety is undoubtedly the great number of individuals which represent it in certain parts of Africa. Not that one finds in any part entire armies of lions, such as are spoken of by the author of an old work, " Voyage à l'île de France ; " but every traveller has had occasion to note that on such a night, in such a place, many lions, roaring horribly, were prowling round his camp fire.

Listen to Le Vaillant :—

" On all sides we heard wild beasts, and above all lions, crying and roaring in a fearful manner. Many of the latter in particular would come and prowl round our camp all night, filling with dismay both my men and my animals ; neither our fires nor our muskets would drive them away ; they would reply with a sort of savage fury to the roaring of those in the neighbourhood, as if inviting them to the carnage by making a

"THEY HEARD HIM BREAKING THE BONES OF THE ANIMAL."

[*Page* 69.

general attack upon us. Nevertheless, daybreak would deliver us."

Mr. Moffat was on a tour among the Barolongs: they had halted beside a pool of water, and at night they lighted the camp fires. Scarcely had the traveller got into his waggon to pass the night, when he heard the oxen stamping their feet with fright. A lion had just followed a heifer which they had neglected to tie up, and carried it off to a distance of about a hundred yards. They heard him breaking the bones of the animal, which was sending forth most lamentable cries. They fired several times in the direction of the noise, and the lion replied only by roaring. Once he even came up to the waggons, two natives having flung fire-sticks at him. The sight of the fire only served to redouble his fury. He was rushing on them, when a ball struck the ground close by him, and he turned away, still roaring.

As the fuel was getting very low, they profited by the temporary departure of the lion to go and seek some wood. "I had not gone far," says Mr. Moffat, "when I perceived between myself and the horizon four animals, whose attention seemed to have been aroused by the noise which I had made in breaking some dry branches. Looking at them more closely, I perceived that these new visitors were no other than lions. I immediately beat a retreat, crawling on my hands and knees towards the pond, to inform our guide of the danger we were in. I found him not less frightened than myself, and looking fixedly in the opposite direction ; there, indeed, were two more lions and a cub, devouring us with their looks, and appearing only to await our movements, in order to decide upon their own. By an optical illusion which I have often noticed in obscurity, they appeared to be double their real size. We lost no time in entrenching ourselves in the waggon and in raking up our fire, whilst at only a short distance from us we could hear the first lion tearing and devouring his prey. When one of the other famished animals, which was prowling about the outskirts, attempted to approach him, he would drive him away with such a horrible howling, as made our poor oxen tremble, and was by no means reassuring to ourselves. We had too good ground to fear that out of six lions there might be at least one which would spring upon us without allowing himself to be stopped by our miserable fire. The two Barolongs begrudged the animal his succulent repast, and from time to time a sigh of regret would escape from them, at the thought of the loss of their cow and of all the milk with which she would have supplied them. A little before daybreak, having swallowed the whole animal, the lion retired, leaving nothing behind but some remains of the bones.

" When the morning arrived we examined the place, and we found from the traces of the lion that he was of the largest size, and that he alone had devoured the heifer. The footmarks of the other lions did not approach within thirty yards of the place. Two jackals alone had come to finish the *débris*. Although I had often heard spoken of the enormous quantity of food which a hungry lion would devour, it required nothing less than such a demonstration as this to convince me that a single individual was capable of devouring all the flesh of a heifer, without counting a large quantity of bones ; for there only remained a rib or two and even many of the marrowbones had been broken, as if with a hammer."

Livingstone says, " Whilst I was engaged in removing our dwelling to Kolobeng, there came such a large number of lions round our half-deserted homes, that the natives, who remained with Mrs. Livingstone, would not have dared for the world to go out of doors after nightfall."

We could multiply examples almost without limit.

The author whom we have just quoted observes somewhere, that the abundance of lions is explained by that of the large game ; and of this latter he gives us in many places of his book marvellous examples. I cannot resist the pleasure of citing the following passage :—

" The valley named Kandchy, or Kandehāi, is as picturesque a spot as is to be seen in this part of Africa. The open glade, surrounded by forest trees of various hues, had a little stream meandering in the centre, A herd of reddish coloured antelopes stood on one side, near a large baobab, looking at us, and ready to run up the hill, while gnus, tsessbes, and zebras gazed in astonishment at the intruders. Some fed carelessly, and others put on the peculiar air of displeasure which these animals sometimes assume before they resolve on flight. A large white rhinoceros came along the bottom of the valley with his slow sauntering gait without noticing us ; he looked as if he meant to indulge in a mud bath. Several buffaloes, with their dark visages, stood under the trees on the side opposite to the pallahs."

And again : " At a short distance below us we saw the Kafue, wending its way over a forest-clad plain to the confluence, and on the other side of the Zambesi ; beyond that lay a long range of dark hills. A line of fleecy clouds appeared lying along the course of that river at their base. The plain below us, at the left of the Kafue, had more large game on it than anywhere else I had seen in Africa. Hundreds of buffaloes and zebras grazed on the open spaces : and there stood lordly elephants, feeding majestically, nothing moving, apparently, but the proboscis.

"When we descended we found all the animals remarkably tame. The elephants stood beneath the trees, fanning themselves with their large ears, as if they did not see us at 200 or 300 yards' distance. We saw great numbers of red-coloured pigs (potamochoerus) standing gazing at us in wonder.

"The number of animals was quite astonishing, and made me think that here I could realize an image of that time when Megatheria fed undisturbed in the primeval forests."

III.

ANOTHER very characteristic feature of the dog-nosed lion, is that individuals of this species often unite together for the purpose of hunting large game.

"In winter, during the daytime, one frequently sees," writes Delegorgue, "bands of lions united together for the purpose of encircling and driving the game towards gorges and wooded passes difficult of access, where some of their number are posted. These were regular but noiseless *battues*, the scent of the lions being quite sufficient to drive away the herbivorous animals that came across it. On two occasions, and at only a few minutes' interval, we had fallen into the centre of a line of these beaters; there were twenty at first, thirty afterwards. A rhinoceros appeared to be the chief object of their greed."

Livingstone has seen a herd of buffaloes defending themselves against a number of lions with their horns, the males in advance, the females and their young forming a rear guard.

Messrs. Oswell and Vardon were riding along the banks of the Limpopo, when a waterbuck started in front of them. "I dismounted," says Mr. Vardon, " and was following it through the jungle, when three buffaloes got up, and, after going a little distance, stood still, and the nearest bull turned round and looked at me. A ball from the two-ouncer crashed into his shoulder, and they all three made off. Oswell and I followed as soon as I had reloaded, and when we were in sight of the buffalo, and gaining on him at every stride, three lions leapt on the unfortunate brute. He bellowed most lustily as he kept up a running fight, but he was of course soon overpowered and pulled down. We had a fine view of the struggle, and saw the lions, on their hind legs, tearing away with teeth and claws in most ferocious style." Three to one is an evident proof of weakness, and even three of the South African lions together are not always able to master a buffalo, especially a female with little ones to defend. A traveller reports having seen a female, backed by a river, hold five lions in check, and compel them to beat retreat. "I have heard from a good source," says Sparrman, "of a lion being knocked down and trampled to death by a herd of cattle which, pressed by hunger, he had dared to attack in the daytime."

It is scarcely fair, however, to exaggerate the relative weakness of this animal. He has been seen at the Cape to seize a heifer and carry her off with the legs trailing the ground, with as much ease as a cat would carry a mouse, leaping without any difficulty across a ditch, with his load in his mouth.

Two farmers who were out hunting saw one of these lions carrying away a buffalo from the plain over a woody hillock; certainly the animal had had the sagacity to lighten the body by disembowelling it.

How do they manage to share the plunder in these expeditions made in common? With a certain degree of equity, one is compelled to think, since the habits of association continue. When an old male conducts the band, as he reserves to himself the chief part of the work, he gives to the others his leavings; and if this is not charitable, it is just. This is the way in which the affair is managed, as described by a native:—

"When several lions together come upon some game, the oldest of the troop crawls towards the object of their covetousness, whilst the others lie down quietly on the grass. If he succeeds in becoming master, as he usually does, he leaves his victim and retires for a quarter of an hour or so to take breath; during this time the other lions approach and lie down at a respectful distance. When the chief has finished his repose, he begins an attack on the brisket and the abdomen; and after helping himself to the most succulent morsels, he takes another rest, none of his companions in the meantime dreaming of moving. Then, when he has finished his second repast and retired, the others, having watched all his movements, pounce upon the remains, which are soon devoured.

"On other occasions, when a young lion has seized his prey and an old one passes by, the young one stands aside until his senior has dined."

Observations made by Mr. Moffat, in continuation of his account of the night attack already mentioned, agree entirely with the foregoing recital.

The same native saw one day a lion creeping towards the stump of a tree of a blackish colour, and not unlike a human form. When the animal had approached within about twenty-five yards, he sprang forward, and missed his mark by a foot or two, which appeared to mortify him very much. After smelling the object and discovering his mistake, he returned, all ashamed, to his starting-point, made another leap with no more success, began again, and at last, at the fourth attempt, he succeeded in planting his paw on the imaginary prey. Then, satisfied with himself, he went away.

Another Hottentot relates that a troop of zebras was going along a straight path leading to the margin of a precipice. A fine stallion formed the rear guard, when suddenly, from a rock ten or twelve feet high, a lion sprang at the stallion and missed him. The path wound round the rock, and the lion comprehended that if he could scale it at a single bound, a second spring would bring him on to the back of his victim. He made the attempt, but could only get sufficiently high to see the zebra galloping away, beating the air with his tail. He then made a second leap, and a third, until he succeeded. During this time two other lions had arrived, and chatting together after their fashion, the old lion made them take a turn round the rock; then, leading them to the starting-point, he made the leap once more in their presence, to show them what must be done in future on a like occasion.

"They were evidently talking together," said the African, "but being in a low tone of voice I could not comprehend a word of their conversation; and fearing that they might take a fancy to exercise their art at my expense, I silently retired, leaving them in the midst of their deliberations."

IV.

The Hottentots hold that a lion never kills a man at once, when he has struck him down, unless he is irritated by resistance. This would appear to be true in general, for there is nothing absolute in natural history.

A father and his two sons were pursuing a lion, when the animal turned upon them, and springing upon one who fell underneath him, the others, without losing an instant, fired and killed the lion, whilst the young man was found to have sustained no injury.

A farmer of the name of Botta, who was also a captain of militia, was seen in the same position as this young man. For a long time the lion crouched over him. The man at length extricated himself, with only a few bruises and a bite in the arm—deep, certainly, but not such as to put his life in danger.

We have also the testimony of Livingstone. He had wounded a lion, and was in the act of reloading his gun, when the lion sprang upon him. "I was upon a little height; he caught my shoulder as he sprang, and we both came to the ground below together. Growling horribly close to my ear, he shook me as a terrier dog does a rat. The shock produced a stupor similar to that which seems to be felt by a mouse, after the first shake of the cat. It caused a

sort of dreaminess, in which there was no sense of
pain nor feeling of terror, though quite conscious of
all that was happening. It was like what patients
partially under the influence of chloroform describe,
who see all the operation, but feel not the knife. This
singular condition was not the result of any mental
process. The shake annihilated fear, and allowed no
sense of horror in looking round at the beast. This
peculiar state is probably produced by all animals
killed by the carnivora; and if so, is a merciful provision by our benevolent Creator for lessening the pain
of death. Turning round to relieve myself of the
weight, as he had one paw on the back of my head, I
saw his eyes directed to Mebalwe, who was trying to
shoot him at a distance of ten or fifteen yards. His
gun, a flint one, missed fire in both the barrels. The
lion immediately left me, and attacking Mebalwe, bit
his thigh. Another man, whose life I had saved
before, after he had been tossed by a buffalo, attempted
to spear the lion while he was biting Mebalwe. He
·left Mebalwe and caught this man by the shoulder,
but at that moment the bullets he had received took
effect, and he fell down dead."

It would seem that the lion takes quite another
course when the victim is a beast. Most frequently
he kills him at a blow. A farmer had just unyoked
his oxen, when a lion threw himself successively on

two of these animals, whose deaths were instantaneous.

He had broken their spines.

Whence comes this difference?

Doubtless from the fear which man inspires, and the natural prudence of the lion, which makes him always suspect some trap on the part of man, especially of a white man, even when he has him in his clutches.

All Africans are agreed as to the distinction which the South African lion establishes between the white man and the negro.

"One morning," relates Mr. Moffatt "after having passed the night at the door of the cabin in which slept the principal man of the village and his wife, I told them that I had heard something moving on the other side of the hawthorn hedge, under the shade of which I had been sleeping; and I concluded that some of the cattle had broken loose during the night. 'No,' replied my host, 'I have seen the trail this morning—it was the lion.' And he added that some nights previously this lion had broken through the . hedge at the very place where I had been sleeping, and had seized a goat, which he carried off through the other side of the enclosure. Then he showed the remains of a mat, which he had taken from his cabin, and burnt to frighten the animal.

"I asked him how it happened that he had arranged

for my sleeping just on that particular spot. 'Oh!' said he, 'the lion would never have had the audacity to leap on you!'"

It would doubtless be scarcely wise to trust absolutely in that; but since the lion can learn to fear man, one can understand that he would have more respect for a white man than a black one.

As to the lion's caution, it is so great, that to him who only knew him from this side of his character, he would seem to be the most pusillanimous of animals.

One of the horses belonging to Mr. Codrington, an Englishman who was travelling in Africa, having broken loose, he was caught in his flight by the trunk of a broken tree, round which the bridle had become entangled, and he was found on this spot forty-eight hours afterwards.

All around him were to be seen numerous footmarks of lions, but the horse was safe and sound. Evidently this animal, thus fastened in the open country, was to them a very suspicious object; they believed in a trap, and did not venture to make the attack. Livingstone says:—" Two lions came up by night to within three yards of oxen tied to a waggon, and a sheep tied to a tree, and stood roaring, but afraid to make a spring, fearing a trap. On another occasion one of our party was lying sound asleep, and unconscious of danger, between two natives behind a bush at Mashue; the fire was nearly out at their feet, in consequence of all being completely tired out by the fatigues of the previous day. A lion came up to within three yards of the fire, and there commenced roaring instead of making a spring : the fact of their riding ox being tied to the bush was the only reason the lion had for not following his instinct and making a meal of flesh. He then stood on a knoll three hundred yards distant, and roared all night; and continued his growling as the party moved off by daylight next morning."

———

V.

THIS natural cautiousness and this acquired fear seem to us to explain perfectly the conduct of the lion in the circumstances we are about to relate.

A man belonging to the congregation of Bethany was returning home from visiting a friend : he made a détour in order to pass by a little spring, where he hoped to find an antelope for his family supper. When he reached this spot the sun was already very high, and not finding the game he was in search of, he placed his gun against a rock, quenched his thirst, returned to the rock, and smoked his pipe, and then slept.

Soon afterwards, roused up by the intense heat of the

"HE STRETCHED OUT HIS HAND TO SEIZE HIS GUN." [Page 83.

sun, he observed an enormous lion lying down within three yards of him, and with his eyes fixed upon him. After remaining for some minutes motionless with terror, he recovered his presence of mind, and looking round for his gun, he stretched out his hand to seize it.

The lion saw the movement, lifted his head, and roared terribly. The man made one or two further attempts, but the gun being beyond his reach he gave it up; for the lion, who appeared perfectly to understand his object, also exhibited signs of anger whenever the poor wretch moved his hand.

The position soon became intolerable; the rock on which the man was lying had become so heated by the sun, that his naked feet could not bear the contact, and he was obliged constantly to change them, by placing one over the other. The whole day passed in this manner, then the night, without the lion moving from his place; the sun rose again, and soon the intense heat on the rock rendered the poor Hottentot's feet insensible.

At noon the lion arose and went towards the spring, looking behind him to watch the movements of his prisoner; and seeing him stretch out his hand towards his gun, he turned round in a fury, and appeared as if he was about to spring upon him. After having appeased his thirst, he returned to his post near the rock.

Another night passed away. The man, when he recounted this scene, said that he was ignorant as to whether he had slept or not; but that if he had slept it must have been with his eyes open, for he had never for one moment ceased to see the lion at his feet.

In the afternoon of the following day the lion returned to drink at the spring; and there, having heard some noise which frightened him, he disappeared in the wood.

The man went for his gun; but when he stooped to pick it up, his ankles refused to sustain him, and he fell down. With his gun in his hand he dragged himself to the spring; his great toes were shrivelled, and the soles of his feet scorched.

He waited a short time for the return of the lion, resolved to shoot him through the head, but the animal did not come back; and 'fastening his gun behind him, he crawled as well as he could on his hands and knees into a neighbouring path, happily just as a friend was passing, who carried him into a safe place, and bestowed on him all the care which his state required; but he lost his toes, and remained a cripple for the rest of his life.

An old Hottentot returning to his home perceived a lion that he thought was following him: at the end of an hour or so he no longer doubted it—the lion was following. He naturally thought that the animal was only waiting for the night, in order to spring upon him. The situation was a critical one; for, on the one hand, the poor wretch could not reach his village before night, and, on the other, he had no other weapon than a stick.

Trudging along, not without turning his head round from time to time, our friend pondered what was the best thing to be done, without being able to find a satisfactory solution. The country was absolutely naked—not a tree or refuge of any kind at hand. At length an idea occurred to him.

In those parts there are frequently found rocks, sometimes of a considerable height, which on one side are connected with the surrounding land by a very gentle slope, whilst on the other they rise to a peak, and form a precipice: they call them *kliprons*.

To find a klipron became the fixed idea of the old Hottentot; and, turning aside from his path, he soon found one, which sloped gradually upwards. He gained the summit, and reaching the verge, he sat down, his legs hanging over the precipice, and looked behind him. The lion was standing still, and watching this very doubtful manœuvre.

They remained thus, the man sitting, the beast standing, until night came on. Then the Hottentot quietly slid down to a projection on the vertical face of the rock; and, standing upright, he quickly placed his hat and his mantle on the end of his stick, raised it above his head and above the rock, and waited.

He had not long to wait. During these preparations the lion had stealthily crept up. He saw the mannikin, and, supposing it to be the Hottentot, he sprang, and fell head foremost down the precipice. Then the poor fellow shouted, " *T'katsi! t'katsi!*"—an interjection which combines within itself a thousand curses.

" We saw two large lions," says Sparrman; " the one had a mane, and was therefore a male. They were at a distance of from two to three hundred yards from us, in a little valley; and the moment they perceived us they took to flight. They used in running a kind of sidelong motion, like certain dogs, interrupted by occasional light springs; with their necks slightly elevated, they seemed to be looking at us sideways. I was very curious to study them more closely; and we followed on horseback, shouting after them, and tempting them to stop.

" These cries caused them to redouble their speed; and when they reached the river, which we had to cross, they plunged into the neighbouring thicket, and we lost sight of them."

A rich peasant, Jacob Kok, of Zée-Koe-rivier, was one day walking in his fields, with a loaded gun, when he saw a lion at a short distance from him. He took aim, but his gun hung fire; and, full of fright, he fled for his life, followed in turn by his game. Soon finding himself out of breath, he leapt on a heap of stones, and, facing round, resolved to defend himself with the butt end of his gun.

This attitude imposed on the lion; he stopped and sat down with the coolest air in the world. Nevertheless, the hunter did not dare to move. In running he had lost his powder-flask, and he could only await the pleasure of the lion. They remained in this position for a good half-hour, looking at each other; after which the lion skulked slowly away, affecting some dignity meanwhile, but, when he had gone some distance, he bolted away with all his speed.

A man, meeting a lion unexpectedly, fell down fainting from fright. The lion, astonished, peered round the bush, and seeing no one, suspected an ambuscade, and started with his tail between his legs.

He would have gone more slowly if he had been perfectly certain of being seen, for his vanity equals his distrust.

"In the daytime," says Livingstone, "the lion stands a second or two gazing at the person he encounters; then he turns slowly round, and walks as slowly away for a dozen paces, looking over his shoulder; then he begins to trot, and when he thinks himself out of sight, bounds off like a greyhound."

Mr. Moffat says that he has seen bushmen, and even women, compel a lion to leave the prey which he had just seized, simply by shouting and making a noise.

But this portrait ceases to be a correct one when the lion is very hungry or has charge of young ones. The cry of the stomach drowns the voice of prudence; the lion no longer distinguishes between black and white; and in a man he only sees a possible prey or a certain enemy.

" At Lopepe, a lioness sprang on the hind-quarter of Mr. Oswell's horse, and when we came up to him we found the marks of the claws on the horse, and a scratch on Mr. O.'s hand. The horse, on feeling the lion on him, sprang away, and the rider, caught by a wait-a-bit thorn, was brought to the ground and rendered insensible: his dogs saved him."

Mr. Codrington, too, was attacked in the same way, though not hunting the lion at the time; but turning round, he shot him dead in the neck.

A widow woman was living in a very isolated dwelling with her two sons, the eldest of whom was about nineteen years old. One dark night they were awoke by the lowing of the cattle enclosed in a yard at a short distance. They ran for their arms. It was a lion. He had broken through the palisade and made horrible carnage amongst the cattle. Neither the Hottentots nor the young men themselves dared to

enter the enclosure, but the intrepid widow went in
alone armed with a gun. In the darkness she could
scarcely see the lion, but she fired nevertheless; the
wounded animal rushed upon her and threw her down.
At the cries of the poor woman her two sons ran to her
assistance; they found the lion attacking his prey.
Furious and desperate, they rushed upon him, and
slaughtered him on the bleeding body of their mother.
Besides the deep wounds which she received in the
throat and on different parts of her body, the lion had
bitten off her hand, which he had devoured.

All help was useless, and the same night she expired,
in the midst of the sorrows and vain regrets of her
children and the assembled servants.

After a successful expedition against the bushmen,
who had stolen some cattle, Le Vaillant returned to a
spot where the evening before he had left two Kami-
nouquois, who had served him as guides. "Just as
we were approaching, I heard from the troop ahead
such frightful cries as almost froze my blood with
alarm. I ran up immediately, and saw a frightful
spectacle, the picture of which haunts me to this hour.
Those two unfortunate savages, who so generously had
offered to conduct me, were lying on the ground,
almost dead, and weltering in their blood.

"My first idea was that they had been murdered by
some of those belonging to the horde we had been

pursuing, but on approaching nearer I was soon dis-
abused.

"One of them had his lower jaw smashed, and almost
entirely gone; the shreds which still remained and
discovered the tongue were hanging all bleeding down
the neck and bosom. He gave no other sign of life
than a slight pulsation; but the prodigious swelling
of his head, the horrible alteration of his countenance,
his eyes out of their sockets, had so greatly disfigured
him, that he preserved no human features, and revolted
my sight at the same time that he lacerated my heart.

"His companion had many bites and tears on his
body, and his arm broken, or rather crushed, in several
places. Nevertheless his state was by no means so
grievous, and he could even speak. We inquired the
cause of his misfortune. He told us that after we had
quitted them, they extinguished their fire in order not
to be discovered by the bushmen, and whilst sleeping
at a few yards from his companion, he was in a short
time woke up by his cries. He at once rushed to his
assistance, and he found himself fighting against the
claws of a lion, which he wounded in the flank. But
the animal, feeling himself wounded, threw himself
upon him, and before fleeing away, reduced him to the
state in which we found him."

VI.

THE natives hunt the lions with guns or lances, which-ever of these weapons they may chance to possess. Each of these arms was in use in the encounter which we give below, and which nearly proved fatal to Dr. Livingstone.

"The Bakatla of the village Mabotsa were much troubled by lions, which leaped into the cattle-pens by night and destroyed their cows. They even attacked the herds in open day. This was so unusual an occurrence, that the people believed they were be-witched—'given,' as they said, 'into the power of the lions by a neighbouring tribe.' They went once to attack the animals, but being rather a cowardly people, compared to Bechuanas in general on such occasions, they returned without killing any.

"It is well known that if one in a troop of lions is killed, the others take the hint and leave that part of the country. So the next time the herds were at-tacked, I went with the people in order to encourage them to rid themselves of the annoyance by destroying one of the marauders. We found the lions on a small hill about a quarter of a mile in length, and covered with trees. A circle of men was formed round it, and they gradually closed up, ascending pretty near to each other.

"Being down below on the plain with a native schoolmaster, named Mebālwe, a most excellent man, I saw one of the lions sitting on a piece of rock within the now closed circle of men. Mebālwe fired at him before I could, and the ball struck the rock on which the animal was sitting. He bit at the spot struck, as a dog does at a stick or stone thrown at him; then leaping away, broke through the opening circle and escaped unhurt. The men were afraid to attack him, perhaps on account of their belief in witchcraft. When the circle was reformed, we saw two other lions in it, but we were afraid to fire lest we should strike the men; and they allowed these beasts to burst through also. If the Bakatla had acted according to the custom of the country, they would have speared the lions in their attempt to get out. Seeing we could not get them to kill one of the lions, we bent our footsteps towards the village. In going round the end of the hill, however, I saw one of the beasts sitting on a piece of rock as before, but this time he had a little bush in front. Being about forty yards off, I took a good aim at his body through the bush, and fired both barrels into it. The men then called out, 'He is shot! he is shot!' others cried, 'He has been shot by another man too; let us go to him!' I did not see any one else shoot at him, but I saw the lion's tail erected in anger behind the bush, and turning to the people, said,

'Stop a little, till I load again.' When in the act of ramming down the bullets I heard a shout. Starting, and looking half round, I saw the lion just in the act of springing upon me."

This was the occasion on which Livingstone was knocked down, and, as it will be remembered, the lion quitted him to throw himself on the other aggressor: this one was bitten on the thigh. "Another man," he continues, "whose life I had saved before, after he had been tossed by a buffalo, attempted to spear the lion while he was biting Mebālwe. He left Mebālwe and caught this man by the shoulder, but at that moment the bullets he had received took effect, and he fell down dead. The whole was the work of a few moments, and must have been his paroxysm of dying rage. In order to take out the charm from him, the Bakatla on the following day made a huge bonfire over the carcase, which was declared to be that of the largest lion they had ever seen. Besides crunching the bone into splinters, he left eleven teeth-wounds on the upper part of the arm."

To see Europeans at the work, let us now return to that buffalo which had started up at the approach of Messrs. Oswell and Vardon, and which we left at the moment when three lions were upon him tearing him with their teeth.

" We crept up within thirty yards, and kneeling down

blazed away at the lions. One lion fell dead almost on the buffalo; he had merely time to turn towards us, seize a bush with his teeth, and drop dead with the stick in his jaws. The second made off immediately; and the third raised his head, coolly looked round for a moment, then went on tearing and biting at the carcase as hard as ever. We retired a short distance to load, then again advanced and fired: the lion made off, but a ball that he received *ought* to have stopped him, as it went clean through his shoulder-blade. He was followed up and killed, after having charged several times."

The colonists generally hunt the lion on horseback. But they only hazard themselves on the plain. They go two or three together, in order to help each other in case of need, and if the game holds to any cover they send dogs in to induce it to show itself.

The attitude of the lion is very different according as he sees the hunters are near or at a distance. In the first case he flies with all his speed; in the other he moves to and fro with a fierce air, but without permitting himself to seem in the least trouble. When sharply pursued he soon slackens his .pace, and at length stops, faces his enemies, shakes himself, and utters a short roar. This is the moment for action. The nearest hunter fires, and if he has missed his mark, or only wounded the lion, he gallops off; then comes the turn of the second, and in case of need of the third; and then, if this is not enough, the two first, who have by this time reloaded their guns, again enter the lists; and so they continue until the lion is at last obliged to acknowledge himself vanquished.

It is said that there has been no instance of a colonist paying the price of his life for the pleasures of this sport.

It is, however, not merely a pleasure; it is an absolute necessity for those who live in the remote parts of the colony, as they have to defend their cattle against the attacks of this insatiable marauder. "They are always eager for the chase," says Sparrman: "the peasants with whom I was hunting seemed only to long for an encounter, quite regardless of any possible danger likely to happen to them—from which, indeed, they felt themselves quite secure."

Le Vaillant tells of a widow who kept house by herself, and who, when wild beasts came to alarm her flocks, would mount on horseback, pursue them vigorously, and never give in until she had either killed them or driven them away from her canton.

We have seen the part which dogs bear in this sport — sometimes, indeed, they really do all the work. Twelve or fifteen of the dogs bred by the Cape farmers will perform wonders. When the lion sees them approach, his pride prevents him from going away; he sits down and waits for them. Then the dogs surround him, and rushing on him all at once, they commence tearing him to pieces. They rarely give him time to strike more than one or two blows with his paws, each one of which, however, is sure and certain death to two or three of his assailants.

The natives sometimes dig pitfalls for lions, as carefully concealed as possible; but it very rarely happens that the cautious animal is caught therein.

A traveller asserts that the following stratagem succeeded:—"They place," says he, "the figure of a man near to some guns, disposed in such a manner that they will discharge themselves into the body of the animal the moment he springs on the mannikin. As this method is as easy as it is sure, and as they are not particularly anxious to take the lions alive, the colonists rarely put themselves to the trouble of laying pit-hole traps for them." There are, however, not wanting instances in which lions have discovered this mine.

"A lion," continues the same traveller, "had broken through the bars of a gateway into a walled enclosure in which the cattle were kept, and committed great ravages there. The people of the farm, not doubting but that he would return by the same way, bristled the entry with loaded firearms attached to a cord stretched across the gateway, and feeling quite satisfied that he could not enter without disturbing them. The lion returned a little before nightfall. He had probably some suspicion of this cord : he examined it with his paw, and, without exhibiting the least fear of the artillery roaring in his ears, entered boldly, and devoured the prey which he had left the previous evening."

To conclude this subject, we will describe the siege of a thick brake of underwood, in which a whole family of lions had taken up their domicile. An entire horde of Hottentots were on foot, armed with spears and other weapons. Even the women and children had joined the party—not to fight, but to look on. Le Vaillant commanded the expedition. The following is an abridgment of his account of the adventure :—

"The thicket was about two hundred yards long by sixty wide. The space it occupied was lower than the surrounding land, so that to penetrate into it we had to descend. It was composed mostly of thorn bushes, with some mimosas which rose towards the centre.

"In the impossibility of attacking the two formidable beasts in their entrenchment, it became a question as to the best method of getting them out of it. I decided to place my marksmen, at short distances apart on the heights all round the wood, in such a manner that the lions could not gain the plain without being seen, being persuaded that as soon as we could get them into the open country we should find ourselves the strongest, and should not be long in gaining the victory.

"When we were all at our posts, oxen were driven in advance, and by dint of shouting and lashing we forced them into the thicket. At the same time my dogs began to bark; and in order to frighten the lions and compel them to come out, pistols were frequently discharged. The oxen, on scenting the enemy, fell back in terror, and rushed towards us; but, driven back by our clamouring, by the barking of the dogs, and the noise of our arms, they became furious, striking against each other and bellowing in a fearful manner. The lions, on their part, were now growing angry, and exhibited their rage by horrible roars. We heard them successively in all parts of the thicket, without their daring to show themselves anywhere. The collision of two opposing armies is not more clamorous than were their defiant roarings, confounded as they were with the animated shouts of the men, the noise of the dogs, and the furious bellowing of the oxen. This frightful concert lasted a good part of the morning, and I had already begun to despair of the success of our enterprise, when suddenly I heard piercing cries from the opposite side, immediately followed by the firing of a gun, and at the same time succeeded by shouts of joy. I ran over to the spot, and found the lioness expiring. She had at last sprung out of her stronghold and thrown herself furiously on my troop ; but Klaas had fired and shot her through the body. It was evident from the appearance of her udders that she had young ones, and I was not deceived in my conjectures. It occurred to me to make use of her body to attract them out of the thicket. With this design I caused her to be dragged out and placed at a certain distance, not doubting but that they would follow her scent and approach her, or perhaps that the male would follow, either to avenge her or to defend them.

"But my *ruse* was useless, and we spent several hours in vain waiting for them. The cubs, being disquieted at not seeing their mother, ran growling all round the stronghold ; and the male himself, separated from her, redoubled his angry roars. We saw him for an instant on the outskirt, his eyes on fire, his mane bristling up, and lashing his sides with his tail ; but he was out of reach of my rifle. One of my gunners, posted more advantageously, missed him, and he disappeared. The sun was going down, and we decided to put off the affair until the following day. The following day the three lions had decamped."

CHAPTER V.

The Mufflon.

THE mufflon is one of the mammals most characteristic of the island of Corsica. It is not, however, peculiar to that island; it is also found in Sardinia, in Crete, and in Spain.

In the summer it keeps to the plateaus which border the regions of eternal snow; during the winter it descends lower. In the extreme cold it seeks the deserted cabins in which the shepherds had lodged in the summer; and it is said that in some exceptional winters mufflons have been seen mingling with the horses, mules, and sheep in the stables.

They go habitually in flocks of from five or six at least, to twenty or twenty-five at most, browsing the different kinds of grass, and the young shoots of many kinds of trees and shrubs, those of the ivy above all. Whilst they are feeding an old male keeps sentry on some elevated point; at the least danger the alarm is given, and in the twinkling of an eye all have disappeared in the ravines; and they bound

"AN OLD MALE KEEPS SENTRY." *[Page 101.*

from rock to rock, gaining places so steep that no human foot could reach them.

Important zoological questions have arisen with reference to this animal. It is said that Buffon considered it to be the original stock of the different varieties of the domestic sheep.

"I do not know from my own experience," writes M. H. Aucapitaine, "anything to justify this assertion.

"In Corsica, the country of the mufflon, one ought to be able most easily to discover the connection between this animal and the sheep of the country. Now there seems to be no affinity between these two species, notwithstanding the fact that the Corsican shepherds leave their flocks at full liberty in the higher regions of the mountains, where the mufflons could most easily mingle with the sheep. No cross has ever been observed between these animals, except in exclusive cases when the mufflons were in captivity. Unfortunately, so far as I know, the results of these couplings have nowhere been followed up."

On the other hand, the Prince P. N. Buonaparte writes :—

"The mufflon reproduces itself when in captivity, both with the sheep and the goat. In both cases the mixed breed is prolific. These facts have been many times established, both by ourselves and by many other inhabitants of Corsica ; and they upset the theories of the learned. We can affirm also that the mufflons breed with the gazelle; and a tame stag in the enclosure of our house killed two mufflons which we possessed, *from jealousy.*"

"There are," says the author whom we have just quoted, "three methods of hunting the mufflon: by *caccia piutta*, that is, by surprise. The hunters start some hours before daybreak to gain the heights which command the dales and mountain sides where the game is to be met with. Sometimes they bivouac the previous evening in the immediate neighbourhood, if the wind is favourable. At daybreak they place themselves on the look-out. The mufflons do not move until the sun shines on their pasturage. If the weather is cloudy, they come out later, and are much more distrustful.

"As soon as they are perceived, their position is marked, and the hunters creep near to them, often on their hands and knees, to protect themselves from all accidents of the ground, rocks, trees, or bushes. It is necessary to be to the windward, otherwise every other precaution would be useless; they are off like lightning, before it is possible to get within range of them. By the greatest caution it is sometimes possible to get sufficiently near to shoot them with buckshot. It is always well to load one barrel with a ball, for distant firing, and when the game is still.

" Whatever braggarts may assert—and they are not wanting, even in Corsica—when the mufflon has seen the hunter, it is by the merest chance that he can touch him with a ball. He darts like a flash through everything into the abyss; and if he is wounded he takes refuge in inaccessible crevices, where he dies, and is soon devoured by the eagles and vultures. Often, after many hours, and even days of searching, they come upon him in the most impossible places, by means of ropes and ladders.

" The most frequent method is to occupy the high mountain ridges, by which the mufflons fly the moment they hear the least noise. Some beaters are stationed on the mountain sides, shouting and rolling down blocks of rock with a noise of thunder; and if we are posted to windward, we are not long in seeing the mufflons approach.

" But the best sport that can be made is with one, two, or at most three of the dogs of the country, accustomed to the mountains and the game.

" In winter the mufflons descend to where the snow fails, and they do not pass over that limit unless they are pursued. Ordinarily they are found on the wooded sides of the mountains, or on the open spaces between the great rocks. The hunters follow them into their retreat in the snow, or rather on the borders of it. This is very difficult, for the distance, the frost, and the slipperiness of the descent, cause a delay of several hours in reaching the post of action. On attaining it, a man stationed at the foot of the mountain enters the wood with the dogs, and soon finds the game, which is not slow in giving up possession of the spot to him."

CHAPTER VI.

The Musk Ox.

THIS animal is found in the frozen regions of North America, and particularly—according to Hearne—in the neighbourhood of the polar circle. He is without a muzzle, which circumstance has induced Blanville to separate him from the ox species, and to classify him separately, under the name of *Ovibos*. He is small in size and very low on his legs, and covered with an enormous quantity of wool and dark-brown hair, which in winter reaches almost to the ground. On his back there is a whitish place, which is called the saddle. Large horns, flattened at the base, cover his head like a kind of casque; they are enormous, and are said to weigh almost fifty pounds. It derives its name from the odour which its flesh exhales at certain epochs, and especially at the beginning of spring. This odour is so strong that it communicates itself to the knives with which the flesh is cut up. Excepting in this season, and when the musk ox is fat, his flesh is excellent.

He feeds on grass and moss during one part of the year, and on lichens during the other part.

Notwithstanding the shortness of his limbs, he gallops with great speed, and the facility with which he climbs the mountains can only be compared to that of goats.

In September the musk oxen assemble together in herds more or less numerous, not to emigrate, for Parry has killed many of them on Melville Island, but probably for mutual protection against the wolves, which abound in those parts.

Lieutenant M. E. de Bray relates the following hunt of the musk ox, in a note communicated to *l'Académie des Sciences:*—

" When musk oxen are attacked by hunters, they assemble together, form a very compact phalanx, putting the young animals in the centre, their hind quarters being directed towards the centre, and thus presenting their heads to the enemy in every direction. The males tear up the earth with their horns and fore feet, thus preparing themselves for the combat. One of them, the oldest of the herd, places himself in front, like a general at the head of his army, and advances cautiously to reconnoitre the enemy,

"HE OWED HIS SAFETY TO A LARGE FRAGMENT OF ROCK."

[*Page* 107.

and watching attentively the least movement on the part of the hunters.

"This survey being accomplished, he retires to his post and awaits the attack. Then it is that this animal appears in all his majestic beauty; and when the hunter finds himself for the first time in his presence, he must muster up his courage and strengthen his nerves. But although seemingly so terrible, these animals, either stupid or over-confident in their strength, allow the hunters to approach within a short distance, and then at the first gun-shot the whole herd takes flight, abandoning the dead and the wounded. I have often seen five or six hunters destroy a herd of a score of them. On one occasion only have I seen one of these animals charge; it is true that the poor beast had twelve balls in his body, and being unable to fly, he defended himself to the last moment."

This last story scarcely accords with what Ross relates:—

A musk ox, in whose body he had lodged three balls, threw himself upon him, and the illustrious sailor owed his safety entirely to a large fragment of rock, behind which he took refuge, the animal's head coming in contact with it with prodigious force.

He was eaten raw by the Esquimaux, who on this occasion surpassed even themselves in gluttony.

Filled, but still hungry, they extended themselves on the ground, with their hands full of meat, waiting for a fresh void in their œsophagus, which they at once replenished.

CHAPTER VII.

The Giraffe.

It is to Le Vaillant that we owe our first exact ideas respecting the giraffe, 1783–5.

With what a transport of joy he writes in describing the first giraffe which fell under his hand !

"Pain, fatigue, cruel want, uncertainty for the future, disgust sometimes for the past, all disappeared in presence of this new prey. · I could not withdraw myself from contemplating it. I measured its enormous height. I looked with astonishment from the animal destroyed to the instrument which had destroyed him. I called my people to examine him over and over again ; and although each one of them could have done as much, and although we had slaughtered heavier and far more dangerous animals, yet I had been the first to kill this one; and I was about to enrich natural history, to destroy romance, and in my turn to establish a truth."

This giraffe measured sixteen feet three inches from his hoofs to his head. In general the males measure from fifteen feet to fifteen feet six inches, and the females from thirteen to fourteen feet. They feed on the leaves of trees, particularly of the mimosa, and also on the herbage of the prairies, which they can browse without kneeling down, although the contrary has been stated. But they often lie down, either to ruminate or to sleep, from which cause a considerable callosity is formed on the sternum and on the knees. These animals are peaceable and timid, and in presence of any danger their first movement is to fly. They trot very swiftly, and a good horse can with difficulty keep pace with them. But what a singular gait! perched at the extremity of a long neck, which works in a single piece from the shoulders, the head incessantly sways backwards and forwards, as if the animal were lame. When we see him in front, the anterior part of the body being much larger than the posterior, it is easy to fancy ourselves in front of the trunk of a dead tree.

Although giraffes flee from danger, it is not correct to say that they will make no resistance when the opportunity of flight is closed to them. It is true that their means of defence are but small. Their frontal horny protuberances do not appear to be of any assistance to them. Le Vaillant never saw them use them against his dogs; but they have their feet, and they use them very courageously. The hind quarters are so light, and their kicks so rapid, that the eye cannot follow them; and this means of resistance has succeeded perfectly, even against the lion himself.

A Namaquois came one day in great haste to inform Le Vaillant that he had seen in the neighbourhood a giraffe browsing the leaves of a mimosa tree.

"Full of joy, I instantly leapt upon one of my horses, and made Bemfry mount another, and followed by my dogs, I galloped towards the mimosa indicated; but the giraffe was no longer there. We saw him crossing the plain on the western side, and we spurred on to overtake him. He was trotting along lightly, without, however, exerting himself unduly. We galloped after him, and from time to time fired several shots after him; but imperceptibly he gained so much upon us, that after following him for three hours, we were forced to stop, our horses being quite blown, and we lost sight of him."

This gives an idea of the swiftness of the giraffe.

Another opportunity presented itself on the following day, on which occasion five giraffes were hunted during the whole day, but they effected their escape under cover of the night.

At length, the following day was for M. Vaillant one of the happiest of his life.

"I started on a hunting expedition at daybreak, in the hope of finding some game for provisions.

"After some hours' march, we perceived, on turning

a little hill, seven giraffes, which my dogs at once attacked. Six of them took to flight together. The seventh, cut off by the dogs, started off in the opposite direction.

"Bemfry at that moment was dismounted, and leading his horse by the bridle. In less than a twinkling he was in the saddle, and started in pursuit of the first six. As for me, I followed the other at full gallop; but in spite of the efforts of my horse, he soon gained so much upon me, that in turning a hill he disappeared from my sight and I gave up the pursuit.

"Nevertheless, my dogs were not long in reaching him, and he was compelled to stop to defend himself.

"From the place where I was I heard them giving tongue with all their might; and as their barking seemed always to proceed from the same spot, I concluded that the animal was surrounded by them, and I immediately spurred on towards them.

"In fact, I had scarcely turned round the knoll when I perceived him surrounded by the dogs, and endeavouring by rapid kicks to keep them off. I at once dismounted, and a shot from my rifle brought him down.

"Delighted with my victory, I returned to call my people to flay and cut up the animal. Whilst I was looking about me, I saw Klaas Barter, who, with an air of great earnestness, was making signs to me, which at first I could not comprehend. But, turning my eyes in the direction indicated by his hand, I perceived with surprise a giraffe, under a great ebony tree, assailed by my dogs. I thought this must be another one, and ran towards him. It was the same, which had got up, but which, just as I was about to fire a second time, fell down dead."

This large game was becoming scarce, and the people of our traveller were almost dying of hunger. They shared the animal amongst themselves, first selecting for the master some choice bits, which he ate broiled, and which he found excellent. The thin bones placed on a brazier of hot coals furnished marrow as white and firm as mutton tallow, and was very appetizing. "I had never before seen any so fine, and I regretted much not having any bread to make toast with it. I had a certain quantity of it melted, with which I filled the giraffe's bladder; and this provision served me for a long time in cooking cutlets from the same animal."

But these material necessities could not make Le Vaillant forget the interests of science. We shall be glad to learn the means which he adopted in the midst of a desert in central Africa to prepare the skin of the gigantic animal.

"Klaas," he writes (his factotum), "had swept and levelled a piece of ground about twenty feet square I had the skin spread out there, with the hair underneath, the sides and corners being kept down with large stones.

"I had to dry the skin of my giraffe, to consume the grease, and to destroy all the causes of fermentation, which might rot or damage it. With this design I had great fires made, in order to use the cinders. I spread these cinders on the skin, taking care that it was covered entirely, and quite equally.

"It remained in this state during the whole night; and, lest some hyæna should come to it, under the cover of the darkness, to devour the fragments, I pitched my tent quite close to my treasure.

"The dissection of the head and the hoofs took me the whole afternoon of the following day, because I could not obtain, and, indeed, I did not wish any aid but that of Klaas. The hoofs cost me little trouble; but it was not so with the head. We began upon this by raising the skin from the jaw-bones and cheeks; and by taking away the flesh from underneath, replacing it by tow, to preserve the form. The eyes were treated in the same manner: after having taken out the globe of the eye, and dried its orbit with hot cinders, I filled the cavity with tow, in order to sustain the eyelids.

"The most difficult operation was the extraction of the brain, which in the giraffe is large; and I was the more embarrassed because I desired to extract it without incision or fracture. At last I thought of sponging it out, so to speak, little by little. We managed to do this by the aid of a steel point, furnished at the end with bristles from the *kros* of my Hottentots; and which, thus changed into a pencil, was introduced into the bony cavity of the cranium. I filled the empty cranium with hot cinders. As to the anterior part of the head, from the nostrils to the bony appendages, which in this animal form a kind of horns, I had nothing to do, because, not being fleshy, I had simply to dry it.

"From time to time I renewed the cinders on the skin; I even kept up great fires for many days together, solely for the purpose of having these cinders. They operated at once by the combined action of their desiccative and alkaline property; and this method succeeded admirably."

This skin was brought to Europe; and Le Vaillant expressed his regret at not having an apartment sufficiently high to exhibit the animal, and to offer to amateurs a true model of what the animal is in nature.

Let us transport ourselves now to the other extremity of Africa—Nubia.

Five or six men, mounted on good horses, plunge into the desert, accompanied by camels carrying water and provisions. When they discover their prey they separate, and, shouting aloud, they manœuvre in such a manner as to drive him towards a wood. The animal, hoping to get out of their sight, is not slow in falling into the trap. He plunges in amongst the trees, seeks the thickest part of the wood, but the bushes and the branches hindering his progress, the hunters gain upon him ; and, as if the natural obstacles were not enough, they stretch cords across the path of the giraffe. He falls, and they throw a halter over him. If he refuses to walk, they kill him, in order at least to obtain his skin. This is an extremity to which they are never reduced with the young ones : more docile than the adults, they follow the hunters, who sell them in the neighbouring villages.

But the giraffe has other enemies besides man. There is the lion.

If the giraffe is vigorous, he sometimes succeeds in escaping from him. A traveller relates having seen two whose shoulders bore indelible marks of their having carried the monarch of the forest on their backs, and that they had come off victorious from the struggle. The lion always endeavours to throw himself on the giraffe's back ; plunging his sharp claws into the shoulders, he gnaws before him until he reaches the vertebræ of the neck, then the two animals fall together, and the lion is often maimed in the struggle ; and sometimes even worse luck befalls him.

A young savage in South America, returning to his village, stopped at a spring to quench his thirst; then lying down on the bank, he fell asleep. Awakened by the hot rays of the sun, he perceived through a bush a giraffe browsing on the leaves of a mimosa, and at a few yards' distance a lion, motionless, watching the giraffe, and preparing to spring upon him. He at length made his spring, and, with a gigantic bound, threw himself towards the head of the animal. The giraffe quickly leaped aside, and so cleverly, that the lion fell on his back into the middle of a thorn-bush. The giraffe immediately scampered off, and the negro was not slow in imitating him, not doubting but that the lion would soon be on his footsteps.

Some time afterwards eagles were seen wheeling round above the mimosa. On search being made the carcase of a lion was found, extended on a bed of thorns.

CHAPTER VIII.

The Tapir.

Tapirs have the general form of the hog, but they are distinguished from it at first sight by a little fleshy proboscis, susceptible of being lengthened out or withdrawn. This proboscis is not like that of the elephant, an organ of prehension.

There are many species of the tapir. One called the American Tapir, is common enough in the hot countries of South America. Another is met with in the most elevated regions of the Cordilleras, and the Andes. A third inhabits the forests of the island of Sumatra, and the peninsula of Malacca.

The American Tapir, seen on the borders of rivers, hides itself during the day in the midst of the thickest bushes, and seeks its food, which is entirely vegetable, at night. It has a preference for water-melons and citrons. It goes but a very small distance from the spot where it has established its dwelling. It is a very timid animal, and the least noise frightens it; and it seeks out the most profound solitudes.

Notwithstanding this wild disposition, it is tamed with the greatest facility—at least, if it is taken young. Its timidity soon makes way for the greatest familiarity. "It becomes tame from the first day," says d'Azara, "and goes all about the house without leaving it. Every one can touch it and stroke it—not that it prefers one to another, or obeys one more or less than another; and if it is wished to get it out of a place, it becomes necessary to force it out. It does not bite; and if it is inconvenienced in any way, it utters a shrill kind of whistle, quite disproportionate to its size. It drinks like the hog, and eats raw or cooked meat and food of all kinds, and whatever comes in its way—not excepting woollen rags or bits of silk. I have seen it many times gnawing my walking-stick; and on one occasion it was doing the same to a silver snuff-box. It seems to be more gluttonous than the pig, and its sense of taste does not seem to enable it to distinguish one thing from another."

A contemporaneous observer, M. Chabrillac, does not agree with d'Azara as to the indifference which, according to this latter, the tapir shows for the persons amongst whom it lives. "It loves the society of man," says M. Chabrillac, "attaches itself to all those who show it kindness, and exhibits a special predilection for children, whose sports it shares without ever doing them the least harm."

He gives a very convincing proof of the attachment of the tapir:—"I have kept for two years a tapir which had been taken when young on the banks of the Rio San Francisco. He passed all the time of his captivity in the court of a college frequented by two hundred scholars, with whom he played like the most intelligent dog, without ever offending even those who sometimes took pleasure in teasing him. When the hour of recreation arrived, he would appear delighted, showing his pleasure by leaping and racing about. If the scholars did not seem to be paying proper attention to him, he would go to excite and entice them to come and share in his gambols. But when he was too much tormented by his playfellows, far from seeking to defend himself by doing them any injury, he would run to take refuge in a trough filled with water for his use, and there, uttering a grunt of satisfaction, he appeared to set his persecutors at defiance, whilst they, tiring of the game, would leave him in repose, and soon give themselves to other sports. This interesting animal, which as a rule ate nothing but green herbs, had become accustomed to all kinds of nourishment. They gave him all the *débris* of the kitchen, which he ate without his health appearing to suffer in the least degree. He died of a wound in his leg, caused by a fall upon a broken bottle."

An inhabitant of Santa-Maria-de-Belene (Para) pos-

"IF HE CAN REACH DEEP WATER, HE PLUNGES IN."

[*Page* 121.

sessed a very familiar tapir. Having given him to the captain of one of the Brazilian coasting vessels, he took him himself on board. But when the tapir saw his master depart, he began to show signs of disquietude. At length, when the steam was getting up, the animal became furious, ran about from one side to the other, and having found a port-hole open, he threw himself into the sea, swam towards the coast, arrived there safe and sound, and went to find his master, who vowed he would never part with him again.

They hunt the tapir by night, sometimes with dogs, sometimes by lying in wait for him in the water-melon grounds; but as he has excellent sight, and a very sensitive ear, it is not easy to surprise him.

If he can reach deep water he throws himself in, and remains a long time submerged, and reappears at a long distance from the place where he plunged in. When there are woods in the immediate proximity, ho throws himself into the thickest brakes, removing and breaking whatever comes in contact with his head, which he carries close to the ground.

Those who hunt him with the gun, never stop him at once; and d'Azara relates having seen one whose heart was pierced by two balls, and which before falling ran a distance of two hundred yards. Reduced to extremity, he kicks out his legs and seizes the dog by the back, and shakes them so vigorously that he lacerates their skin.

It sometimes happens at daybreak that hunters on horseback encounter a tapir belated in the open country. The lasso soon stops him in his course, and his fate is sealed; for although he is much swifter than at first sight he seems, he cannot for any length of time compete in speed with a horse.

D'Azara says that the Indians of Paraguay eat the flesh of the tapir; but he adds, that by no means proves that it is delicate; and Barren, in his "*Histoire Naturelle de la France Equinoxiale*," writes, "His flesh is coarse and of a disagreeable taste." We have changed all that.

"The flesh of the tapir," says M. Chabrillac, "is much esteemed in the country where I have had occasion to eat it very often, and I can assert that it yields in nothing, both for savour and nutritive qualities, to the best meat we have in Europe. When smoked, it keeps a long time, and acquires a flavour which would be appreciated by our most delicate *gourmets*."

M. Victor Bataillo writes from Guyana:—"I have often eaten the flesh of this animal. Without being delicate and of the first quality, it is good, and has nothing disagreeable to the taste.

"It has also, since 1818, taken a very important

place in the food of the colony, particularly of the labouring classes.

"Before 1848 they did not hunt the tapir much. The Indians alone gave attention to this sport, because the Europeans and the slaves were occupied in other works. Since the emancipation the hunt has been taken up very actively and with success, not only amongst the Indians, but near the city, in the environs of which the animal is by no means rare. I have very frequently seen them killed at a distance of one or two leagues from the city. Not a week passes in which two or three are not brought in ; and these are cut up and sold retail, like butcher's meat. The price is from 5d. to 6d. per pound, and its consumption is a real advantage to the colony."

The *pinchaque* tapirs are those of the Cordilleras. They inhabit by preference the cold regions, whilst the lower region is frequented by the common tapir : otherwise their habits very much resemble those of the latter. In their nocturnal expeditions they ordinarily go in file, and thus form tracks across the woods, of which the hunters often avail themselves, and which the Indians pompously call royal routes.

These beaten paths are found in regions between 1,400 and 4,400 metres above the level of the sea. The *pinchaques* resort to lonely spots, where the soil is composed of a clayey kind of slate. This slate clay bears the mark of their teeth.

D'Azara also reports that the common tapir eats nitrous earth, and says that he has found a great quantity in the stomach of one of these animals.

Hunters are sure to find the *pinchaques* on these slate-clay spots a little before sunrise, provided they have not been disturbed, for they are very suspicious animals. They will abandon entirely a place near which the country people have laid snares, with all precaution possible, in which they hope to take them.

An encounter with them is never dangerous, and we have only heard of three instances in which they have shown any signs of courage.

A *pinchaque* pursued by dogs faced round upon them on reaching some water, and as this menacing attitude intimidated the first hunter who presented himself, the tapir ran at him, and threw him head over heels.

The other instances are reported of two females, when accompanied by their young ones, which they thought to be in danger. They each upset her man. One of these men had taken the liberty of touching the young tapir with his umbrella.

Once in the water, the *pinchaque* remains there as long as he fancies that he is pursued.

It is related of one, that rather than quit the stream, he allowed himself to be killed with large stones, which the hunter dropped on his head.

One morning at eight o'clock, at the foot of the Peak of Thoma, on the shore of the Combaymee, in a place situated at 1,918 metres above the sea-level, and called *las Juntas*, M. Goudot started up a young female *pinchaque*, which threw itself immediately into the water. Surrounded by dogs, which for the most part kept to the shore, the animal remained for a long time motionless in the midst of the torrent, confining itself to lifting its trunk now and then above the water, and uttering cries which the noise of the stream and the barking of the dogs almost drowned. The dogs, which, in order to reach it, had plunged into the water above the place where the *pinchaque* was, were for the most part submerged, but they were not otherwise hurt. The *pinchaque* came to the top of the water with the greatest facility. A ball passed through its *aorta*, near the heart. After this mortal blow, it had sufficient strength to cross the stream.

The flesh of this animal is red, like that of the bear, and is excellent eating.

CHAPTER IX.

The Hippopotamus.

I.

Sparrman, accompanied by some farmers and Hottentots, had gone for the second time to hunt the hippopotamus: his first attempt had proved unsuccessful. This new enterprise took place in the night, and the method adopted was that of lying in ambush.

Our adventurers were divided, in order to multiply the chances of an encounter. Sparrman, accompanied by two colonists, father and son, was posted on a dry portion of the bed of a river inhabited by hippopotami. A European, and the son-in-law of one of the colonists, occupied a second post, and the natives a third. Sparrman and his two companions had behind them the banks of the water-course, which at that spot were very high. The ground was level, and the night sufficiently bright. Moreover, they were on the path made by the hippopotami. All the chances were therefore in favour of the hunters. They sat down and waited. Sparrman, tormented by mosquitoes, had covered his face with his pocket-handkerchief, and, half asleep, was philosophising on the boldness of three frail individuals awaiting "the behemoth of the prophet Job," and on the impudence of the insects which were attacking such heroes.

Suddenly, a hippopotamus came out of the river with the swiftness of an arrow, and dashed into the path, uttering a horrible cry. "*Heer Jesus!*" cries the farmer, firing off his gun; at the roar of the beast the European and the colonist's son-in-law fled. Sparrman himself had not heard the shot, nor had he seen the beast,—or rather, in the darkness he mistook him for a waterspout, caused by a sudden overflow of the river. He threw down his gun, abandoned his two companions, and rushed desperately to a point high enough to escape the water, knocking himself uselessly against the bluff bank of the river. Astonished that he was not submerged, he asked himself if it was not all a dream? He ran to the farmer's son, whom he found asleep with his fists closed, and snoring lustily, and then to the father, who, entangled in a blanket with which he had enveloped his limbs, was tremblingly endeavouring to disengage himself. "What direction has the flood taken?" asked Sparrman. He stood speechless for a short time. "Are you become a fool?" he said at last. Sparrman retorted. In fact he was not convinced of his error until he saw that the farmer's gun was discharged. Happily, the shot—the flash rather than the ball—had caused the animal to turn round and plunge into the water as precipitately as he had come out of it. Here the hunt finished. Our Nimrods passed the rest of the night in laughing at each other, and smoked their pipes whilst listening to the roaring of the lions.

This is all ridiculous enough; but at all events one sees here pictured with *naïveté* the impressions of a novice who for the first time found himself in the presence of a hippopotamus.

II.

An encounter with him on land is not without peril. An instance is related of a hippopotamus which pursued a native for a long time, who escaped from him with the greatest difficulty. But it is only in certain critical moments, when beasts ordinarily timid become dangerous, that the hippopotamus, unprovoked, shows any aggressive disposition; it is otherwise when he has been provoked and wounded,—then he charges upon the hunter with all his force. Where, however, the species has been subjected to a long and active persecution, they lose all self-confidence; this is always the case where firearms are generally used.

In a locality where the introduction of firearms was

still recent, a native fired on a hippopotamus, which he missed, when the latter seized him in his jaws and literally cut him in two. There is less exposure to unpleasantness of this kind when the animal is attacked from behind, seeing that he is so very slow in turning round; and the negroes usually avail themselves of this circumstance.

III.

HIPPOPOTAMI live partly in the water and partly on land. They are only found in Africa, in the Nile and in most of the rivers which empty into the Atlantic and Indian Oceans. They abound chiefly south of the equator and in the interior of Africa. They live in herds during the day, in water, where they sleep and yawn, elevating their muzzles from time to time above the water; at night they come on land to feed, taking always the same path in going and coming. In walking their legs are so short and their paunch so voluminous, that it almost sweeps the ground. The water is their true home. They are seen descending to the bottom, walking and even running on the mud, rooting up the long grasses with their hooked teeth. Salt, in Abyssinia, saw them walking at the bottom of the Tacagé, at a depth of twenty feet. Ere long they ascend to the surface, raise their heads out of the water, and

K

respire obstreperously, spouting from their nostrils a column of water to the height of five feet; but they only do this in localities where they have not been disturbed—on the Zambesi, for example. Elsewhere, and particularly in the rivers of Londa, where active warfare has taught them prudence, they only bring their nostrils to the air, and breathe so gently that their presence would not be suspected were it not betrayed by their footmarks on the shore. The females, when they have little ones very young, come more frequently to the surface than others, because their nurslings cannot remain under the water so long a time as adults. These little ones cling at first to the neck of their mother, then on her back, and soon they follow her to the pasturage.

IV.

ONE morning Sparrman saw a female with her calf advancing towards him on land; the calf was lame, and was walking slowly. The mother received a ball in her side, and threw herself into the water. The young one was taken and secured; he made a great noise, somewhat like a pig when he is being killed. The hunters were very fearful that at these cries the mother would come out of the river, as had happened to Le Vaillant, who had shot a young hippopotamus

"ON THE RIVER BANK THE MOTHER SHOWED HERSELF."

[Page 131.

and broken its thigh. "But we had scarcely reached it," he writes, "than at a few yards distance, on the river bank, the mother showed herself, and with fearful roars ran towards us, her terrible jaws wide open. This sudden and unexpected apparition so terrified us, that we thought of nothing but flying as quickly as possible; and to prevent any impediment to our speed we even threw down our rifles. For my part, I did not hesitate a moment in doing so with mine, which, being discharged, was useless. The mother, having recovered her young one, did not attempt to follow us, but returned with it peaceably into the water; and her retreat permitted us to go and pick up our guns."

Returning to Sparrman and his captive: this calf was three feet six inches long and two feet high. According to the conjectures of the Hottentots, it could not be more than two or three weeks old. It soon showed signs of a disposition to sociability; but the Hottentots, who have a special liking for its flesh—which, in fact, is agreeable and wholesome, and very like beef—did not give him time to become perfectly tame.

<hr>

V.

THE lameness of the young hippopotamus mentioned above leads us to say, that it is very common to find amongst the animals of this species individuals bearing the traces of considerable wounds. It frequently happens, indeed, that they fight furiously. A traveller was witness to a duel between two males, which he records thus :—

"It was broad day; and, hidden on the river bank, I had been watching for some time the gambols of a herd of these animals, when all of a sudden two of the largest rose to the surface, and rushed at each other. Their great and hideous jaws were extended wide open, their eyes flaming with rage, each one seeming bent on the destruction of his enemy. They seized each other with their jaws; they stabbed and punched with their strong tusks—by turns advancing and retreating, now at the top of the water and sometimes at the bottom of the river. The waves were stained with their blood, and their furious roars were frightful to listen to. They showed very little tact in their movements, but on the other hand they exhibited piggish obstinacy in maintaining their ground, and frightful savageness in their demeanour. The combat lasted for an hour. Evidently they were mutually operating upon armour too hard to admit of their wounds being very dangerous. At last one of them turned his back on his enemy and went away, leaving the other victorious and master of the field of battle."

VI.

Notwithstanding the abundance of hippopotami in certain water-courses, instances of aggression on their part are very rare.

Mr. Moffat, whilst crossing a river, was pursued by a furious hippopotamus, snorting terribly. It may be said, in passing, that the snorting of males can be heard at a distance of a mile. Our traveller escaped with very great difficulty, and if he had been an instant longer in reaching the bank, he would have been a dead man.

Ordinarily canoes circulate in the midst of them without being disturbed. A European was sailing on a river, amongst a number of hippopotami. The canoe passed over one of them. The animal moved away, uttering a significant growl.

A short time ago we read the following, in the recent correspondence of a traveller in Egypt:—

"We remarked on the ground numerous traces of the steps of hippopotami. It was evident that we were in a part much frequented by them. We soon noticed on the river a kind of black floating island; it was the back of an immense hippopotamus. We afterwards saw a second and less voluminous one. Our boats were now approaching, and when they passed near the two backs, the sailors shouted in a peculiar manner, and we saw the hippopotamus first plunge, and then make a sudden spring almost out of the water, exhibiting the body, even to the hind legs. They explained to us that this was a family of hippopotami, which was taking its promenade in the river, and that the mother, believing her young ones were attacked by the boats, had thus elevated herself above the water to see her enemies, and if needful to defend herself."

Here is another picture, taken from the banks of the Kafoué, which is rich in hippopotami :—

"In the ignorance of firearms in which they live, these hippopotami are so little timid that they pay not the least attention to us; the young ones, not much larger than turnspits, and mounted on their mothers' necks, look at us between their ears, and do not appear in the least disturbed by our presence."

This is the case most frequently; here, however, is a slight variation :—

"About mid-day a hippopotamus struck against the front of our canoe, and almost capsized it. The force of the blow precipitated Mashaouana into the river; the rest, of whom I was one, made for the shore, which was about fifteen yards off. The hippopotamus remained on the surface of the water, looking curiously at the canoe, as if forming an estimate of the amount of damage she had done. It was a female whose young one had been killed the evening before with a javelin. We were eight in the canoe, and the violence of the shock which she had given us was ample proof to each of us of the enormous strength of the animal which had produced it. Except Mashaouana's ducking, and the bath which all had to take, no other damage was done by the accident. It is such a rare thing to be attacked by one of these animals, when the precaution is taken of sailing near the shore, that my companions cried spontaneously, ' The beast is mad ! ' "

Here is another, and still more marked instance. M. Knoblecher, head of the Austrian Catholic Mission on the White River, reports, that in one of his voyages his boat separated a female hippopotamus from her young ones. The mother in a fury rose above the water, just at the same moment that M. Knoblecher's cook was leaning the upper part of his body over the side: the poor fellow was seized, and disappeared under the waves, carried away by the enormous beast.

It is not the less true that the principal danger incurred by travellers is not to be imputed to intention on the part of the hippopotamus.

The most frequent risk is that of being capsized by the pressure of an animal, in rising from the bottom to the surface without crying " Look out ;" still it most frequently happens that the sailors come off

at worst with a ducking. Sometimes, nevertheless,
the pachydermatous brute returns in a fury, and
destroys the capsized boat.

VII.

WE have said that in its nocturnal movements the
hippopotamus constantly follows the same path. The
hunters profit by the custom, and this is the way they
take them in the Soudan :—

Two of the party stand near the path, in the most
likely spot; they are armed with lances, with a hook
at the end like a fish hook, to which is attached a cord
eight or ten yards long, at the other end of which is
a wooden float; others go in front of the animal where
he feeds. They frighten him by shouting, beating
drums, and brandishing lighted torches. The alarmed
hippopotamus returns to the river, and the nearest
hunter throws his barbed javelin into his flanks. The
wounded animal carries the dart into the water, and
the very rapidity with which he flies contributes to
increase his wound by the resistance of the float.

This piece of wood, which floats on the surface, also
enables the hunter to watch the evolutions which the
amphibious animal performs under the water. Nevertheless, it sometimes happens that it is difficult to
follow it in the night-time. To overcome this incon-

venience as much as possible, the hunters divide themselves into several groups, and if they lose the animal during the night, they easily find him in the daytime. The hippopotamus, exhausted by his struggles, by loss of blood, and want of food, soon comes to die near the shore, unless the hunters in their boats have in the meantime killed him with the lance; but it sometimes happens that he drags a float for many days, especially when the harpoon has been badly planted. M. Tremaux one day encountered a hippopotamus thus pierced.

"Whilst we were still being towed by the people of Lony, I heard a shout, 'The hippopotamus! the hippopotamus!' I surveyed the liquid surface, expecting to see the monstrous head and back of the animal; and I was astonished not to see anything. I observed on the water a kind of Greek cross, formed by two short pieces of wood strongly fixed and bound together in the centre. This cross was cutting through the water, and floating swiftly down the stream, making the water foam, as if moved by some invisible power. As it neared us the float appeared to be agitated in an extraordinary degree, and at the same time a formidable snorting, mingled with the noise of the rippling water, was heard close to the boat. We perceived a hippopotamus, which, frightened by the boat, near which he unexpectedly found himself, gave a great spring half out of the water, and then plunged in again, dragging the float with great fury.

"A short time afterwards some men hailed us from the shore, inquiring if we had seen the hunted water ox."

In Abyssinia they hunt the hippopotamus with guns. Salt gives an account of one of these hunts, which was not a very successful one.

"Placed on an elevated and prominent rock, we were not long in perceiving, at a distance of about sixty feet, a hippopotamus, which, without any signs of fear, exhibited his enormous head above the water, and sniffing violently somewhat in the manner of a porpoise. Three of us fired at him, and he was thought to be struck in front; he looked up, groaning and roaring angrily, and immediately plunged. We expected to see his body floating on the surface of the water, but he reappeared at the same place more cautiously, and without appearing to be at all disconcerted by what had already happened to him.

"We fired again, with no more success than at first. We continued to fire on many other animals, but I am not certain that any one of them was wounded. Our leaden balls were too soft to penetrate the skulls of these great animals—they continually rebounded. Nevertheless, towards evening they became more circumspect; they confined themselves to merely exposing their nostrils above the water, spouting it into the air by the force of their breathing.."

The most common mode of hunting in South Africa is also with the rifle. In the regions visited by Le Vaillant, Sparrman, and Livingstone, they also dig pits in the paths followed by the animal. M. du Chaillu tells us, on the contrary, that the employment of this trap is unknown on the Gaboon.

He thus relates one of his hunts:—

"There was here a place in the river shallow enough for them to stand in and play around; and here they remained all day, playing in the deep water or diving, but for the most part standing on the shallow, with only their ugly noses pointed out of the water, and looking for all the world exactly like so many old weatherbeaten logs stranded on a sand-bar. We approached slowly and with caution to within thirty yards of the school, without seeming to attract the slightest attention from the sluggish animals: stopping there, I fired five shots, and, so far as I could see, killed three hippopotami. The ear is one of the most vulnerable spots, and this was my mark every time. The first shot was received with but little attention, but the struggles of the dying animal, which turned over several times and finally sank to the bottom, seemed to rouse the herd, who began to plunge about and dive down into deep water. The blood of my victims discoloured the water all round, and we could not see whether those which escaped were not swimming for us.

"Presently the boat received a violent jar, and looking overboard, we perceived that we were in the midst of the herd. They did not, however, attack us, but were rather, I imagine, anxious to get away. We, too, pulled out of the way as fast as we could, as I was not anxious to be capsized. Of the dead animals we recovered but one, which was found two days after on a little island on the river's mouth. I think it likely that the negroes secretly ate up the others as they washed ashore, fearing to tell me lest I should claim the prizes.

" I afterwards determined to go on a night hunt after hippopotami. We lay down under shelter of a bush and watched. As yet none of the animals had come out of the water. We could hear them snorting and plashing in the distance, the subdued snort-like roars breaking in upon the still night in a very odd way. The moon was nearly down, and the watch was getting tedious, when I was startled by a sudden groan, and peering into the half-light, saw dimly a huge animal looking doubly monstrous in the uncertain light. It was quietly eating grass, which it seemed to nibble off quite close.

" Igala and I both took aim; he fired, and without waiting to see the result ran away as swiftly as a good pair of legs could carry him. I was not quite ready, but fired the moment after him; and before I could get ready to run, in which I had not Igala's practice, I saw there was no need to do so; the beast tottered for a moment, and then fell over dead."

These results are very different from the ineffective shots of Sparrman.

Le Vaillant, met with success equal to that of M. du Chaillu. An old Namaquois spoke to him one day of the trouble he was in.

"He was only a short distance from the river. Hippopotami swarmed there; his companions and he had wished to take some from time to time for their food; but although they had dug pits and laid traps along the shore, they had only succeeded in taking three animals during the two years they had dwelt in the canton.

"The animals, he said, were too sharp for them; and he did not doubt but that, with my guns, the effect of which he had heard, I might kill as many as I pleased.

"My plan was to start in the afternoon of the same day, to pass the night near the river, and to begin the hunt on the following day at dawn. I took with me all my hunters. A detachment of the horde followed me, with some baggage oxen to carry the produce of our sport; and at day break we were all in active motion.

"One half of the troop crossed the river by swimming, whilst the other half remained on my side When the swimmers reached the other shore they separated into two bands, one of which went up the river, at a short distance from it, and the other descended. The same was done on my side. The four bands thus embraced three-fourths of the river space; I alone remained in my place in the centre of the hunters. At a given signal all had orders to leave their posts slowly and to come towards me, some shouting as loud as they could, others firing their guns at intervals, in order to drive up any hippopotami that might be found in that space of the river to within range of my gun. They encountered eight, and all the bands of hunters being reunited in one common centre, nothing further was wanted but patience and dexterity.

"In a short time we wounded several of them. Two were already dead, and the people of the horde were transported with joy. But some amongst them having swum out in order to bring to land the two dead beasts, one of the swimmers received from a wounded hippopotamus a blow with his snout, and another had his thigh ripped open by his tusk. This double accident made me fearful of something worse happening. I recalled my people, and, to the great regret of the Namaquois, I terminated a hunt which all said ought to have been more successful, but which could not be continued without very great peril."

CHAPTER X.

The Rhinoceros.

One traveller says that the sight of a rhinoceros is sufficient to put a lion to flight. Another, without contradicting the first, says that the rhinoceros makes the lion fly like a cat; and a third writes,—"He kills even the elephant, by tearing open his belly with his tusk." A fourth says,—"Men are the only enemies whom he fears, and this fear ceases when he is wounded or pursued."

Listen again to another one :—"He is at once a traitor and an aggressor whom nothing frightens, and a furious brute whom all resistance only renders the more implacable." This animal inhabits both Asia and Africa.

There are always degrees of character, and thus it appears that the white rhinoceros is relatively gentle and confiding. This mildness, however, must not be exaggerated. A white rhinoceros, having been wounded by Mr. Oswell, threw both horse and rider into the air with one blow of its tusk.

What might one expect after that from the polite-
ness of the black rhinoceros ?

Dr. Livingstone writes :—" Mr. Oswell was once
stalking two of these animals, and as they came
slowly to him, he, knowing that there is but little
chance of hitting the small brain of this animal by a
shot in the head, lay, expecting one of them to give
his shoulder, till he was within a few yards.

" The hunter then thought that by making a rush to
his side he might succeed in escaping ; but the rhinoceros, too quick for that, turned upon him, and, though
he discharged his gun close to the animal's head, he
was tossed in the air. My friend was insensible for
some time, and on recovering found large wounds on
the thigh and body. I saw that on the former part
still open, and five inches long."

Mr. Moffat having brought down a black rhinoceros,
the natives threw themselves on the beast, shouting
with joy ; twelve lances at once penetrated the sides of
the victim. The punctures reanimated him; he sprang
up in an instant, and, tearing up the earth with his
horn after his fashion, rushed upon his conquerors,
who promptly showed him their heels.

The rhinoceros is, after the elephant, the largest
mammiferous animal known on the earth. The name
is derived from two Greek words, which might be trans-
lated *horn on the nose.* It is well known, in fact, that

"THE HUNTER WAS TOSSED IN THE AIR."

[Page 144

the frontal nasal region is surmounted, in adults, with one or two horns, according to the species.

They live on vegetables, and their dental system is perfectly suited to this kind of food. Their neck is so short, and so little flexible, that they are much less fond of grass than of browsing the leaves of branches within their reach, which their very mobile and triangular pointed upper lip easily seizes According to Chardin, the Abyssinians tame the rhinoceros, and make him work like an ox.

It rarely happens that more than four or five are met with at once, and it is pretty well to encounter one. They are hunted on account of their flesh, which is considered a great treat by the savages.

In Nubia they hunt him on horseback, the men being entirely naked.

They throw themselves on him, and irritate without being able to wound him.

In spite of their dexterity and the agility of their horses they do not always escape the blows of their formidable enemy. The infuriated animal pursues his assailants. Then one of them detaches himself from his companions, and pretends to wait for him. The rhinoceros turns his rage on this one, and abandons the other hunters, who, moving off rapidly, seek a favourable place near some large tree, chosen before-hand.

When the horseman who had remained behind, engaged with the animal, supposes that his comrades have attained their retreat, he starts off like a dart, reaches the foot of the tree indicated, leaps from his horse, which gallops off, and climbs swiftly up the branches.

The rhinoceros, which has followed him, dashes furiously against the tree, as if he meant to upset it, and strikes his horn deeply into it. But whilst he is making unheard of efforts to disengage himself, the hunters in ambush fall on him and kill him with their lances. As to the horse, he stands still when he finds that he is no longer pursued, and, attracted by the neighing of his companions, he is not slow in rejoining them.

The rhinoceros, when attacked, takes voluntarily, as we have seen, a tree for a hunter, and discharges his rage on the former. Livingstone attributes this blundering to the fact of the horn being so placed as to obstruct the line of vision; and he gives as a proof that the variety named *Kua-baōbo*, having the horn projecting downwards, and therefore not interfering with the sight, was able to be much more wary than its neighbours. Be this as it may, the eye at all events is very small, and sunk in the head. On the other hand, the senses of hearing and smell are very subtle; at the least noise the animal takes alarm, pricks its ears, rises up, and listens, that is, if he is not asleep, for his sleep is very heavy.

This has been contradicted, but Sparrman relates as follows :—"Two of our Hottentot marksmen perceived through the bushes, at a distance of three or four yards, a rhinoceros, lying on his right side, and sleeping so profoundly, that he did not wake up even at the loud noise which they made by chance in striking the guns one against the other. Their first movement was to take aim at him; but as he did not awake, and as they could only see the back part of his body, after a short consultation they made a circuit, and placing themselves in a position to point their guns towards the animal's head, they discharged their two barrels at once into his brisket.

" As the animal struggled somewhat feebly, they had little fear that he would as yet wake up and pursue them; then, as much for their amusement as precaution, they recharged their guns and fired several balls into him."

Le Vaillant says that two rhinoceroses had stopped side by side in a plain at a little distance from his camp; he started at once, accompanied by his men.

" One of the two being much larger than the other, I took them to be male and female.

"They were holding their noses to the wind, and consequently presented their croups to us.

"It is a habit of these quadrupeds, when thus stopping, to place themselves to windward, in order to be warned by scent of any enemies they have to fear. Occasionally, they turn the head to cast a glance behind, to watch for their safety, but it is simply a glance, and the affair of an instant.

"We were discussing the disposition to be made for the attack, when Jonker, one of my Hottentots, begged me to allow him to attack the beasts alone. I permitted him to do so. He stripped naked and departed, carrying his gun with him, and crawling on his belly like a serpent.

"During this time I placed my hunters in the posts they were to occupy, whilst I remained where I was with two Hottentots—the one held my horse and the other the dogs. We were all three concealed behind a bush. I had in my hand an opera-glass, with which I had often watched the *jeu des machines*, and the effect of theatrical decorations: but the objects were changed now! At this moment it exhibited to me two frightful monsters, turning their hideous heads now on this side, now on that. Soon their movements of observation and of fear became more frequent, and I feared lest they might have heard the motions of my dogs, which, having perceived them, were struggling to escape from their keeper, and to rush towards them.

"Jonker, on his part, continued to advance, though slowly, keeping his eyes fixed on the two animals, and becoming suddenly motionless the instant they turned their heads in his direction. His crawling, with all its interruptions, lasted for an hour. At length I saw him direct his movements towards a great tuft of milk-wort, which was within about 200 yards of the rhinoceroses.

"Arrived there, and sure of being well concealed, he arose, and after turning his eyes on all sides, to see that his comrades were at their posts, he prepared to fire.

"During the whole time of his crawling I had followed him with my eyes, and in proportion as he advanced, I felt my heart palpitate involuntarily. But the palpitation redoubled when I saw him so close to the animals, and on the point of firing at one of them. What would I not have given at that moment to have been in Jonker's place, or at least beside him! I waited with the most vivid impatience for the shot to be fired, and I could not conceive what prevented his firing; but the Hottentot who was by my side, and who with his naked eye could distinguish him as perfectly as I with my *lorgnette*, said that if Jonker did not fire, it was because he was waiting for one of the rhinoceroses to turn, that he might aim at his head.

"At last, the largest of the two having turned his head in our direction, he fired.

"Wounded with the shot, he uttered a frightful cry, and, followed by the female, ran with fury towards the place whence the noise had come. A cold perspiration came over me, for I expected to see the two monsters break through the bush, crush under their feet the unhappy Jonker, and tear him in pieces; but he had thrown himself flat on the ground, and the *ruse* succeeded perfectly. They passed near him without seeing him, and came straight towards me.

"Then my agony was turned into joy, and I prepared to receive them. But the dogs, already excited by the gun-shot which they had heard, became so maddened at their approach, that being unable to hold them, I unloosed them and let them on them.

"At this sight they took a turn, and made off in the direction of one of the ambuscades, where they underwent another firing; then in a third direction, where again they were met with another shot. My dogs harassed them beyond measure, which still increased their rage. They kicked at them furiously,— they tore up the plain with their horns, and ploughed up furrows seven or eight inches deep, throwing around them a shower of stones and pebbles.

"During this time we were all approaching, in order to make as close a circle round them as possible, and to bring all our forces against them. This multitude of enemies with which they saw themselves surrounded, threw them into inexpressible fury. Suddenly the male stopped, and ceasing to fly before the dogs, turned upon them to attack and rip them up. But whilst he was pursuing them the female got away.

"I was not sorry for this flight, which was indeed much in our favour, for it is certain, that in spite of our number and our arms, two such formidable enemies would have very much embarrassed us. I must even acknowledge that without my dogs we should not have been able to encounter the risks and perils of the one remaining. The traces of blood which he left on his path told us that he had received more than one wound, which only served to increase his rage.

"Nevertheless, after some time occupied in making his furious attack, he beat retreat, and seemed to wish to gain some bushes, apparently to support himself, and that he might be harassed in front only. I divined his *ruse*, and with the design of preventing it, I ran towards the bushes, making signs to the two hunters nearest to me to go there also. He was not more than thirty yards from us when we gained the post, then all three facing him at the same time, we fired, and . he fell, without being able to rise again."

CHAPTER XI.

The Elephant.

MANY Indians imagine that a human soul dwells in
the elephant's body. In Siam and in Pegu white elephants are regarded as the living manes of Indian
emperors. These animals, exempt from all service, live
in palaces, are served by numerous domestics, eat the
choicest food out of golden vessels, and are clothed
with magnificent ornaments. They must not bend their
knees, except before the emperor, who returns their
salute. Notwithstanding so much adulation, they remain gentle and obedient. If the Indians would take
the trouble to reflect, this last circumstance would
demonstrate to them that elephants are not animated
by human inspiration. They are but beasts, in fact,
but they are the wisest of all beasts. None surpass
them either in intelligence, address, strength, or docility; none leave in the hands of the hunter a spoil
more choice or precious; and hence the motives for
which man declares war on them.

In India the hunting of the elephant has for its end

sometimes to make prisoners, and sometimes to obtain ivory. In South Africa the latter is always the object in view; and for the reason that in India the elephant is employed in war, in hunting, and in a variety of works, whilst in Africa he is not so employed at the present day; besides, the species in this latter region is much smaller and weaker than in the other.

There are two species, the Indian and African. The Indian elephant has a concave forehead, small tusks and ears, teeth formed in serrated laminæ, the number of which rise to twenty-six; five nails to the fore-feet, and four to the hind-feet. It is found all over the continent, from the Indus to the Eastern sea, and in the great islands of Southern Asia.

The African elephant has a rather convex forehead, large tusks, which attain eight feet in length; ears so vast that they cover a large part of the shoulder. The teeth are formed of ten laminæ only; four claws to the fore-feet, and three to the hind-feet. It is found from Senegal and the Niger to the Cape of Good Hope.

The two species live in large herds in solitary forests. One male conducts the herd. When danger menaces them he takes the lead, the females and the young follow. They never attack man or any animal; but when provoked, they defend themselves with intrepidity, and their weight, their speed, and their tusks, make them the most redoubtable adversaries that a hunter could encounter.

II.

THERE is, however, an exception to what has just been said as to the inoffensive character of the elephant. As the male who conducts a herd never allows a rival to approach it, there exists a certain number of solitary old boys, who are sometimes most wicked brutes. At certain seasons they become quite furious, and during a week or two they kill whatever they encounter.

Captain Dunlop gives some instances. . He tells us specially of a solitary elephant in the Doon, known by the name of Gunesh, which belonged to the Government Commissariat. Having killed his keeper, he fled to the jungles, carrying, fastened to his leg, a fragment of the chain which had served to attach him. It was therefore easy to recognize him, and he is said to have killed fifteen persons in fifteen years.

A pedestrian courier of the English postal service, whilst on his journey from Bagdad, with his bag of despatches on his back, was pursued by a "solitary," caught, and crushed beneath his feet.

Whilst the canal of Beejapore was being made, about three miles from Dehra, an elephant, which had hidden behind a bush, rushed on some native workmen. He upset one, and holding the wretch's limbs under his heavy foot, he tore away the upper part of his body, by means of his trunk coiled under the armpits, and continued his route, brandishing this bloody trophy.

Two woodmen employed in felling trees in the jungles of Chandnee-Doon becoming ill, instead of following their fellow-workmen, remained in the hut, in the company of a Brahmin, who was employed in looking after the domestic arrangements of the company. One of these woodmen, wanting some water, went out to a neighbouring spring: he did not return. The second went afterwards, but never came back. In the evening their bodies were found at a few yards from the spring. From the footprints on the soil it was easy to divine how they had perished. Both had been the victims of a " solitary." Their bodies did not exhibit any apparent wounds, only a little dust could be seen on their breasts; but when this place was touched by the hand, 't was found that the bones were completely crushed— a gentle pressure of the beast's foot had extinguished the life of these poor fellows.

III.

Elephants are very numerous in certain parts of Africa and Asia.

"HE TORE AWAY THE UPPER PART OF HIS BODY."

[Page 166.

The hunter whom we have just named was encamped on the shores of the Sooswa. There were a number of elephants in the camp; and towards midnight they showed signs of disquietude, and at first uttered short shrill notes; then they made the jungle resound with their roars, which were almost immediately responded to, first from one point, then from another, till the night appeared to be peopled with their voices.

Every one was afoot immediately. "As we were endeavouring to look into the darkness, we suddenly recognized the presence of a great pioneer tusk-bearer, close to our elephants; then large moving masses in the neighbourhood, which appeared to rise and fall. Sometimes a large opaque body, which we had mistaken for a tree or a bush, and, as such, neglected, would suddenly disappear into space in solemn silence, whilst obscure outlines of arched backs and trunks passed before our eyes, like the phantoms of a dream, which are lost in the night. Suddenly the leader of the herd seemed to take alarm, and we heard a long splashing, during which the elephants were crossing the waves of the Sooswa, from our side.

"There was a gap in the bank of the river near to us, and, as the leaders of the elephants chose this route, we soon saw the whole sombre column glide to the coast from us in a bluish light, as regularly as the images in the slides of a magic-lantern.

"There were, as near as I could manage to ascertain, about seventy of them in the herd; and I remarked here and there the pale light of the ivory."

Such are the pictures which unfold themselves in Asia to the sight of the traveller. In Ceylon they frequently take a hundred elephants or more in one *battue*. So much for India. In Africa a like spectacle is seen. Speke, in the Ounyoro, met a herd of a hundred female elephants; and Livingstone says that there are a prodigious number on the spot where the Zonga empties into the Lake Ngami.

Delegorgue estimated that he was once in the midst of a herd of six hundred. A hunter has even pretended to have seen three thousand at once.

IV.

In India the methods of taking elephants are very varied (we will describe farther on how they kill them); to describe them all would be tedious. It is well known what pomp the Eastern princes were used to display in these expeditions.

One day, as the Count de Forbin, then Grand Admiral and General of the armies of the King of Siam, was assisting at a hunt of this kind, the king asked him what he thought of the magnificent display around him. "Sire," replied Forbin, "seeing your majesty surrounded by all this *cortége*, I imagine that I see the king, my master, at the head of his troops, giving orders and disposing all things for a great battle.

" This reply," he adds, " gave him great pleasure, as I had foreseen it would; for I knew that he loved nothing in the world better than to be compared to Louis le Grand; and, if the truth must be written, this comparison, which went no further than the exterior grandeur and magnificence of the two princes, was not absolutely without justice, there being few spectacles in the world more superb than the public processions of the King of Siam."

The following are the modern methods of hunting. In some places they are pursued with tame elephants, trained for the purpose, and very swift.

When these have come up with one, the hunter throws, with much dexterity, a noose of very stout cord, in such a way that the wild animal finds himself caught by the foot. He falls, and they strap him down before he has time or opportunity for rising. They then fasten him between two strong tame elephants, who beat him with their trunks if he is at all refractory, and compel him to walk with them to the stables.

In Ceylon an elephant hunt is a very important affair. The government assembles a great number of Europeans and Cingalese, who meet in the forest where these animals are to be found. All these hunters form a vast circle, which they gradually narrow, advancing and shouting.

The frightened elephants have but one side to fly, and there is found the "redan," into which they are forced to enter. This redan is nothing less than a great circle of stakes, terminating in a sort of narrow neck; once entered into which the elephants can no longer return. In order to force them to enter, shouts are increased, and burning torches are thrown before their eyes; then their fears are redoubled, and they rush into the trap, which encloses them. The first care after the capture is to tame them.

This is managed by placing one or two tame elephants near the opening, by which the wild ones are made to pass out, tied together, as we have said already. Hunger on the one hand, and blows from the trunks of their docile companions on the other, soon inspire them with resignation.

They are also taken by pitfalls. A path is chosen which is used many times in the year by the elephants, and which probably serves as a route in going from the jungles to some spring in the mountains.

Across these paths several pits are dug of about twenty feet wide and fifteen to twenty feet deep, and which are then covered over with branches and turf.

However admirably these pits may be concealed,

it does not often happen that the elephants fall therein. Not only do they try with their feet with the greatest care any ground that looks suspicious, but they make constant use of their trunks to prove the solidity of the soil, or to clear out of the way everything which appears to hide a trap.

It is not an easy matter to draw an elephant out of one of these pits, and it can only be done by the aid of a tame elephant; otherwise it would be necessary to subdue the animal by hunger before thinking of getting him out.

Any one getting within reach of the trunk of an elephant just taken, would do so at the risk of his life; but, singularly enough, a driver mounted on a tame elephant's neck can approach the novice with impunity, and tighten or slacken the noose round his neck or feet.

The cords placed round the legs sometimes cut them to the bone, and leave marks which endure for the animal's lifetime. No nourishment is given to him for several days. This deprivation of food soon brings down his courage, and then it is that his appointed driver insures the friendly recognition of the elephant by bringing him food and unbinding his limbs.

V.

ONCE appeased, they become very submissive, and are used as beasts of burden; they are caparisoned for hunting and for war; they are made to carry heavy loads, and are obedient to the voice and gesture.

"The Siamese," says Forbin, "obtain considerable services from these animals. They use them almost as domestics, and especially for taking care of the children : they take them up with their trunks and put them to bed and rock them to sleep; and when mamma wants them, she has only to order the elephant to go and bring them to her."

Numerous instances which testify to their intelligence and docility are well known.

Can one believe this, which a Siamese king reported of one on which he was mounted?—"This elephant had not long since a groom who half famished him by depriving him a portion of the food allotted to him. The animal had no other means of complaining but by his cries, and made such a horrible noise that he could be heard all through the palace. Not being able to divine the cause of his crying so loudly, but suspecting the real fact, I gave him another groom, who, being more faithful, and having given him, without wrong, his full measure of rice, the elephant divided it into two parts with his trunk, and when he had eaten one half, he set up his cry again, indicating thereby to all who ran to see what was the matter, the infidelity of the first groom, who acknowledged his crime, for which I caused him to be severely chastised."

Count de Warren relates the following, which took place in India during the Coorg war, at a time when the writer's brigade was engaged in the bed of a dry mountain torrent:—

" This circumstance enabled us to appreciate the intelligence of the elephants, and their usefulness in the mountains. Having reached a point where the bed of the torrent fell in cascades, it became a question as to the mode of raising the guns up the almost vertical declivity of a granite rock, the surface of which the waters had worn and polished. The oxen which drew the cannon gave up the attempt after one or two efforts, and lay down, as they always do in desperate cases.

" It was then determined to send for some elephants of the convoy. Two of the most docile were stripped of their loads and led by their guides to the place where the cannons were left. It was indicated to them by voice and gesture what was expected from their courage ; and the confidence thus shown in them was not misplaced. One of the colossal beasts, placing himself behind a gun, applied the extremity of his trunk to it, and pushing it before him, whilst the cannoneers guided it, sent it up the rocky chasm. A little farther on, the gun having rolled into a ravine, and being upset, the two elephants lifted it up with their trunks, one on this side, and one on that, and replaced it on its carriage."

A still more remarkable fact occurred during the terrible insurrection in India.

" One day, during the march on Lucknow, in the month of March, 1858, by the order of General Outram, three howitzers were taken from the backs of the elephants which carried them on the march, and were placed in a battery on a little eminence, for the purpose of annoying the enemy's flank. One of them bears a celebrated name in India, from his mother, of which he is worthy, as we shall see, viz., Kudabar-Moll.

" As soon as the pieces were in position, the animal placed himself, according to orders, at a few steps behind, and looked on. Soon the greater part of the artillerymen fell, decimated by the musketry of the enemy ; seeing this, Kudabar-Moll II. interposed, and taking the cartridges from the waggon with his trunk, he passed them, one by one, to the few survivors. The moment came when there remained only three Englishmen. These brave fellows succeeded, nevertheless, in reloading the howitzers, but before they could fire them they all fell, mortally wounded.

"'Here, my brave Kudabar!' cried he who held the match. The elephant approached, seized the match, fired the first gun, and was ready to continue the manœuvre, when two companies of infantry came up and dislodged the enemy."

But there is nothing perfect in this world—elephant no more than man; here is one proof among others: —"A male elephant, belonging to the commissariat, was drinking at a stream, which passes through the city of Dehra. An old woman approached to fill her pitcher with water, when the animal, seized with an inexplicable desire for mischief, passed his trunk round the woman, threw her down, and placing her under one of his feet, quietly crushed her, and then began to flap his ears and to drink, as if this little buffoonery had been but an innocent wandering of the imagination."

It sometimes happens that domestic elephants escape, and as we have seen some of these become deserters. Others are not slow in becoming disgusted with their liberty, and come back to service of their own accord. A large female, named Ram-Kullee, celebrated at Hurdwar for her cleverness in calming and training the elephants taken in the traps, fled into the jungles on two or three occasions, and each time came back of her own accord.

VI.

We have described the method of taking elephants in India, let us now show by one or two examples how they kill them.

In the wild gorges of Sewalik two natives, a Brinjara and a Ghoorka, accompanied the hunter, who relates as follows:—" We had just thrown ourselves on the ground, exhausted by the heat and want of water, which is very scarce during summer on the northern side of the mountain chain of the Sewalik, when the silence which surrounded us was suddenly interrupted by the cracking of a broken branch. We advanced gently and silently in the direction indicated by the noise, and came upon a herd of six large and several young elephants feeding. They had no wind of us, although I had taken no precaution in this respect; and, flapping their large ears, they continued to browse the bushes of the bamboos and other trees around them. After having placed the

Brinjara at a safe distance, and ordered the little Ghoorka to keep himself at about twenty or thirty yards behind me with my reserve double-barrelled guns, I began to creep towards the herd with my single carabine. Suddenly a change in the wind caused a number of trunks to be raised into the air. The trunk has a little appendage in the shape of a finger, and in a second each of them was turned towards the bush behind which I was stooping down, as if to indicate the place whence danger might be expected. The herd then began to move off slowly, their frequent encounters with woodmen in the jungles having rendered them less easy to frighten than they would otherwise have been. We did not see any ivory-bearer amongst them; and if the male was not near at hand, the head of the troop would be some great muckna, or tuskless male.

"An enormous female was making her repast amongst the branches of a bush of bamboos, at a short distance in front of me. I crept along under the cover, and arrived within four yards of her before she saw me. I aimed at her temples and fired. I had resolved to hasten to the bottom of the escarpment as quickly as I could, to see the effects of my shot, and as soon as I had fired I ran straight to the place where my Ghoorka was waiting. A fearful *fracas* in the trees followed the sound of my gun, and I perceived the Brinjara flying through the wood in a terrible fright.

" As I was not pursued, I returned to the place whence I had fired, and I saw the elephant lying dead.

" The ball had pierced the skull, but it had but touched the brain, although it weighed four ounces, was pointed with steel, and I had charged with six drachms of powder—equal to about four ordinary charges."

Another example. We are this time in the forest of Dholekote, on the track of a whole herd. The interest of the matter consists in this—that the hunter was mounted on a female elephant provided with a saddle. He had determined to descend as soon as he should be in sight of the game, but he was not slow in discovering that the old paterfamilias, which was armed with respectable ivories, took the alarm like the rest as soon as the hunter descended from his seat; whereas, on the contrary, he seemed to contemplate fearlessly the elephant carrying his two men.

" I determined then, in spite of the many objections of the driver, who doubted that my carabine could stop short an elephant in full charge, to go straight to the old male and to fire at him

"THE OLD MALE STUMBLED, AND FELL ON HIS KNEES."

[*Page* 169.

from the back of my elephant. I had an American rifle, the power of which I was very desirous of proving, and with this gun I fired at the animal's temples, at a distance of forty paces. At that distance I could easily hit the bottom of a wine-glass, and I was therefore perfectly certain that I had struck the place I aimed at; but its calibre was not sufficient, and the patriarch scampered off, followed by four balls from my battery, which I foolishly fired off, in the vainhope of stopping him.

"We then recommenced following the track, assisted here and there by drops of blood. After a pursuit of five miles we discovered that we had changed the route, having lost the wounded elephant and taken that of an elephant which had wandered from the path taken by the troop. We were, in fact, following the fresh footprints of a solitary male, whose meditations we troubled at about ten miles from the place where our first shot had been fired. We were now in the forest of Horawalla, where one is always sure to find elephants at the time when the rice is ripening.

"This time I used my heavy carabine, firing from the back of my elephant at about fifteen paces. My aim was not perfectly certain; the old male stumbled and fell on his knees, but as he roared furiously, it was clear that the brain had not been penetrated. I therefore slipped down, and firing another ball straight into the face of the solitary animal at three yards' distance, I killed him instantly; and climbing upon the enormous carcase, I sat in triumph on my dead enemy."

CHAPTER XII.

Elephants (*continued*).

VII.

IN Africa they hunt the elephant not for the purpose of securing a powerful servant, but to procure his tusks. It is, therefore, by his death that all happy expeditions terminate. There are a great variety of ways of ensuring this result.

Let us pass into Nubia for awhile.

Before all things, it is necessary that hunters should know the daily habits of that which they wish to make their prey, as well as the places frequented by it. This condition being fulfilled, they establish themselves in the thick foliage of the large trees which the elephants browse and being invisible, they await his approach; when the unsuspecting animal, finds himself underneath them, seizing a favourable instant, they plunge their lances into his eyes and jaws. This proceeding might appear very simple: it is very dangerous; for if the animal is only wounded, the tree must be a very strong one that he will not tear up by the root. Woe, then, to the imprudent one, who, calculating distance badly, shall have placed himself on a branch low enough for the animal to reach him. He will die beneath the weight of his intended prey.

Those of the Sennaar are taken in a manner which will interest the reader.

Two men, absolutely naked, mount a horse; they are naked because it is necessary that not the least rag should be caught by the branches of trees or bushes when they fly before their enemy.

One of the riders holds a short stick in his right hand, and with his left he holds the bridle carefully. His comrade behind him is armed with a large sabre, the hilt of which he holds in his left hand. Fourteen inches of the blade are covered with twine, so that he can take this part of the blade in his right hand without risk of wounding himself; and, although the blade may be sharp as a razor, he carries it without a sheath.

As soon as they have discovered the animal browsing, the man who guides the horse rushes straight at him, shouting, "I am such a one; this is my horse, named so-and-so. I have killed your father in such a place, and your grandfather in such another place; now I am going to kill you; you are but an ass in comparison with your father." The rider really believes that the elephant comprehends these words, because, irritated by the noise, he endeavours to strike with his trunk, and instead of saving himself, as he might do, by flight, pursues the horse, which turns round and round him unceasingly. At length the rider, galloping close up to the animal, in passing, lets his companion slip down, who, profiting by the moment when the elephant is occupied with the horse, adroitly gives him a sabre cut over the top of the heel, and cuts the tendon which in man is called the "tendon Achilles."

This is the moment of difficulty, for the rider must at once get behind to take up his companion, who springs up on the horse's crupper. They then follow the other elephants with the utmost speed, if they have separated more than one of the herd, and sometimes they kill as many as three of the same band. If the sabre is well sharpened, and the man strikes with a sure hand, the tendon is entirely separated; if it is not, the weight of the animal soon completes the work. The elephant, no longer able to advance, falls beneath the javelin, and expires from loss of blood.

However clever the hunters may be, the elephant sometimes seizes them with his trunk, and with a single blow felling horse and rider to the ground, he tears them limb from limb, one after the other.

Many perish in this manner. Besides this, during the hunting season the earth is so dry from the sun, that there are numerous cracks, and it is then very dangerous for riding on horseback.

Nevertheless, mention has been made of a man who, regardless of the perils of this sport, had arrived at such perfection, that he acted without the aid of any one else. Let him speak for himself.

"I rub my body with elephant grease, and conceal myself in the neighbourhood of the places which they frequent. I watch them attentively, and when I see one separated from his companions, I approach him cautiously. The odour which I give out prevents the animal from paying any attention to me. I am armed with a sharp-edged sword, and with a vigorous arm I strike the animal on the hind-leg, and as quick as a gazelle I disappear. The blood flows from his wound, and the furious animal utters terrible cries, which make his affrighted companions fly. Irritated by the pain, he strikes the earth with his wounded foot, completes the cut, and falls, overpowered by his own mass, incapable of rising. The elephant is alone, the others having taken their departure; I can then approach him without fear, knowing that he will not be succoured; and, provided that I avoid placing myself within reach of his trunk, it is an easy matter to finish him."

VIII.

LET us now go to the south, our way enlivened by one of the hunting adventures of the unfortunate Captain Speke.

This happened in the Oungoro.

"Some elephants were signalled in the neighbourhood. My comrade and I—our guns ready—discovered a troop of a hundred females, on a plain covered with tall grass, here and there sprinkled with hillocks, clothed with dwarf shrubs. We fired at a dozen at least without killing one of these enormous beasts, and only one seemed inclined to charge. Profiting by the thickness of the grass, I crept within reach of the herd, and sent a shot at one of the largest, which had separated from the rest while browsing. The others, taking alarm, formed a group, and snuffing the air with their trunks simultaneously raised, finished by satisfying themselves from the smell of the powder that their enemy was in front of them. Then, waving their trunks, they came nearer to the place where I lay screened by a bend in the ground.

"When they scented me, their march was at once suspended, and erecting their heads, they surveyed me askaunt from head to foot. The situation was menacing. I could not manage so as to strike one in such a way as that it should fall under the blow, and if I deferred for an instant, both I and my companion would be thrown down and trampled under foot. I hastened to aim at the temple, and the blow not proving mortal, the whole band took flight, and hurried off to the open country more quickly than they came. As, therefore, I could not separate one of the wounded elephants, I gave in, for it seemed to me cruel to hit others in pure sport. On reflection, I thought that I ought to have used more powder; the small size of these animals, compared with the Indian elephants, had deceived me, and I had loaded my gun as if for rhinoceros shooting."

IX.

THE same kind of traps is used in South Africa as in Asia. They cover them very cleverly with branches; but old elephants, at the head of a band, have been known to remove the covering from the pits; and Livingstone says that he has seen them drawing young ones from the pit, into which they had fallen.

Travellers also sometimes fall into them; Le Vaillant, for example, who, by means of repeatedly firing his gun, at last attracted the attention of his people, who delivered him.

M. du Chaillu met with the same adventure amongst the Apingis. The pit was ten feet deep, and it was night.

"For once I thought I was lost—alone, abandoned, during the night in this accursed hole. I expected, moreover, to see some great serpent fall on my head. I shouted with all my might, and I had the good fortune to be heard. My people came, and I got out by means of ropes, which they got in the wood and threw down to me."

An elephant, pursued by Livingstone's people, fell into one of these pits, and there received the javelins of seventy men who pursued him; he nevertheless managed to scramble out of the trap, looking like an immense porcupine. The hunters having no more javelins, ran to Livingstone, begging him to finish the animal; he fired two two-ounce balls without killing him.

There is another method peculiar to this country described by M. du Chaillu. "The natives discover a walk or path through which it is likely that a herd or single animal will soon pass. Then they take a piece of very heavy wood, which the Bakalai call *hanou*, and trice it up into a high tree, where it hangs, with a sharp point armed with iron pointing downwards. It is suspended by a rope, which is so arranged that the instant the elephant touches it—which he cannot help doing, if he passes under the *hanou*—it is loosed, and falls with tremendous force on to his back, the iron point wounding him, and the heavy weight generally breaking his spine."

The mode adopted by the Batongas, and the Ban-yai on the Zambesi, is somewhat like the foregoing. " They erect stages," says Livingstone, " on high trees overhanging the path by which the elephants come, and then use a large spear, with a handle nearly as thick as a man's wrist, and four or five feet long. When the animal comes beneath, they throw the spear, and if it enters between the ribs above, as the blade is at least twenty inches long by two broad, the motion of the handle, as it is aided by knocking against the trees, makes frightful gashes within, and soon causes death. They kill them also by means of a spear inserted in a beam of wood, which, being suspended on the branch of a tree by a cord attached to a latch fastened in the path, and intended to be struck by the animal's foot, leads to the fall of the beam, and, the spear being poisoned, causes death in a few hours."

X.

THE attack with the javelin, in the open country, seems to be more worthy of the true hunter. Living-stone thus describes it :—"·I had retired from the noise to take an observation among some rocks of laminated girt, when I beheld an elephant and her calf at the end of a valley, about two miles distant. The calf was rolling in the mud, and the dam was standing fanning herself with her great ears. As I looked at them through my glass, I saw a long string of my own men appearing on the other side of them. I then went higher up the side of the valley, in order to have a distinct view of their mode of hunting. The goodly beast, totally unconscious of the approach of an enemy, stood for some time suckling her young one, which seemed about two years old; they then went into a pit containing mud, and smeared themselves all over with it; the little one frisking about his dam, flapping his ears, and tossing his trunk incessantly in elephantine fashion. She kept flapping her ears and wagging her tail, as if in the height of enjoyment. Then began the piping of her enemies, which was performed by blowing into a tube, or the hands closed together, as boys do into a key. They call out, to attract the animal's attention,—

> 'O chief! chief! we have come to kill you;
> O chief! chief! many others will die beside you;
> The gods have said it,' &c. &c.

Both animals expanded their ears and listened; then left their bath. As the crowd rushed towards them, the little one ran forward, towards the end of the valley, but seeing the men, returned to his dam. She placed herself on the dangerous side of her calf, and passed her proboscis over it again and again, as if to assure it of safety. She frequently looked back to the men, who kept up an incessant shouting, singing, and piping; then looked at her young one, and ran after it, sometimes sideways, as if her feelings were divided between anxiety to protect her offspring and desire to revenge the temerity of her persecutors. The men kept about a hundred yards in her rear, and some that distance from her flanks, and continued thus until she was obliged to cross a rivulet. The time spent in descending and getting up the opposite bank, allowed of their coming up to the edge and discharging their spears at about twenty yards' distance. After the first discharge she appeared with her sides red with blood, and beginning to flee for her own life, seemed to think no more of her young.

"I had previously sent off Sekweba, with orders to spare the calf. He ran very fast, but neither young nor old ever-enter into a gallop. Their quickest pace is only a sharp walk. Before Sekweba could reach them, the calf had taken refuge in the water and was killed. The pace of the dam gradually became slower. She turned with a shriek of rage, and made a furious charge back among the men. They vanished at right angles to her course, or sideways; and as she ran straight on, she went through the whole party, but came near no one, except a man who wore a piece of cloth on his shoulders. Bright clothing is always dangerous in these cases. She charged three or four times, and, except in the first instance, never went farther than 100 yards. She often stood, after she had crossed a rivulet, and faced the men, though she received fresh spears. It was by this process of spearing and loss of blood that she was killed, for at last, making a short charge, she staggered round, and sank down dead in a kneeling posture."

A traveller thus describes a regular battle, in which 500 men were engaged:—

"The forests here are full of rough strong climbing plants, which you will see running up to the tops of the tallest trees. These vines they tear down, and with them ingeniously, but with much labour, construct a kind of huge fence or obstruction, not sufficient to hold the elephant, but quite strong enough to check him in his flight, and entangle him in the meshes, till the hunters can have time to kill him. Once caught, they quietly surround the huge beast, and put an end to his struggles by incessant discharges of their spears or guns.

"Presently a kind of hunting-horn was sounded, and the charge began.. Parties were stationed at different parts of the barrier, or tangle as we will call it, which had an astonishing extent, and must have cost much toil to make. Others stole through the woods in silence and looked for their prey.

"When they find an elephant, they approach very carefully. The object is to scare him, and make him run towards some part of the barrier, generally not far off. To accomplish this, they often crawl at their full length along the ground, just like snakes, and with astonishing swiftness.

"The first idea of the animal is flight. He rushes ahead almost blindly, but is brought up by the barrier of vines. Enraged and still more terrified, he tears everything with his trunk and feet, but in vain ; and the more he labours, the more fatally he is held.

"Meantime, at the first rush of the elephant, the natives crowd round, and while he is struggling in their toils they are plying him with spears, often from trees, till the poor wounded beast looks like a huge porcupine. The spearing does not cease till they have killed their prey.

"To-day we killed four elephants in this way. The elephants about here have the reputation of holding man in slight fear, and the approach and attack are work for the greatest courage and presence of mind. Even then fatal accidents occur.

"To-day a man was killed. I was not present at the accident, but he seems to have lost his presence of mind, and when the elephant charged with great fury at a crowd of assailants, he was caught, and instantly trampled under foot."

XI.

Hunting with the gun, notwithstanding the superiority of the weapon, is full of peril. This may be judged of by the situation in which Le Vaillant found himself on the occasion of his first elephant hunt.

The animal had received fifteen shots, and he was thoroughly enraged; he had led the hunters into brushwood, interspersed with the dead trunks of fallen trees. The elephant, at twenty-five yards from our traveller, charged him. He ran away, the beast at every instant gaining on the man.

"More dead than alive, it only remained for me to lie down flat behind the trunk of a fallen tree. I had scarcely got there when the animal arrived, leaned over the obstacle, and, himself frightened by the noise of my people which he heard before him, stood to listen.

"From the place where I was hidden I might have shot him. Fortunately my gun was loaded, but the beast had already received uselessly so many shots, and presenting himself to me in such an unfavourable position, that, despairing of bringing him down at one shot, I remained motionless waiting my fate. I watched him, nevertheless, resolved to sell my life dearly if I saw him come back to me. My people, uneasy for their master, shouted for me on all sides. I was careful not to reply, and they, convinced by my silence that they had lost their master, redoubled their cries, and came back in despair. The elephant, frightened, returned immediately, and leaped a second time over the trunk of the tree, at six yards from me, without seeing me : then springing to my feet, burning with impatience, and wishing to give to my Hottentots some sign of life, I sent the contents of my gun into his posteriors. He immediately disappeared from my sight, leaving everywhere on his path sure signs of the cruel state in which wo had placed him."

Pursued by an elephant, on the shores of the Zouga, Mr. Oswell fell from his horse into the midst of a thicket ; he fell with his face turned towards the elephant, which was approaching, and could see the enormous foot of the beast about to fall on his limbs. He moved them, holding his breath, and expecting to be crushed by the hind-feet. The animal passed on without seeing or touching him.

Two colonists, having perceived an elephant, resolved to pursue him. Far from being clever in this chase, it was the first time they had seen an animal of that species. The horses were as little experienced as their masters. Nevertheless, they did not evade the attack. They approached to within sixty yards of the elephant without his appearing to take any notice of them.

Then he moved away, without much haste, doubling the distance between them.

One of the farmers descended from his horse, and falling on one knee, and fixing in the ground his musket-stand, he fired.

Scarcely had he time to remount and turn his horse, when the colossal beast was on his track, uttering such a shrill cry that it seemed to pierce the hunter to the very marrow of his bones. Happily he had presence of mind to turn towards a rising ground, the climbing of which slackened the pace of the elephant. The other hunter seized the moment, dismounted, and fired, then sprang on his saddle again, and spurred off with both heels, having now the terrible game behind him : the tactics which had succeeded with his comrade saved him. The elephant did not fall until he had received the eighth ball.

Another colonist, Claas Volk, being hidden behind a clump of prickly shrubs, flattered himself that he should surprise an elephant. The animal scented him, struck him down with his trunk, and trampled him underneath his feet.

A band of hunters had surprised two elephants, the one a male, the other a female, in the open plain. Not far off were some thick and prickly bushes: the animals fled towards the thicket, and the male was soon under cover, but the female, having been wounded, could not fly with the same rapidity. The hunters, cutting off her retreat, prepared to kill her, when suddenly the male, rushing with fury from his retreat, and uttering frightful cries, threw himself upon them. His aspect at this moment was so terrible that all the hunters, leaping on their horses, fled to save their lives —all except Cobus Klopper, who had wounded the female, and who, standing up with the bridle of his horse passed over his arm, was reloading his gun at the moment when the furious animal came out of the wood. The elephant rushed upon him, driving his ivory tusks into the body of the poor fellow; he afterwards trampled him beneath his feet, then lifting him from the ground with his trunk, he threw him to a great height. Having satiated his vengeance he returned towards the female, caressed her affectionately with his trunk, helped her to rise, sustained with his shoulder her wounded side, and, without paying any attention to the shots which the hunters fired from a distance, he soon disappeared with her in the impenetrable retreats of the forest.

Karol Krieger was an indefatigable and bold hunter. He shot with much address, and often found himself in very dangerous situations. Once, with his companions, he pursued a wounded elephant; the animal suddenly turned round, seized him with his trunk, threw him into the air, and trampled him under his feet. The others, struck with horror, fled without daring to look upon the scene of this frightful tragedy.

They came the following day to perform the last duties to their companion. The elephant had torn the body into pieces and strewed the fragments in the dust: they could only give burial to the scattered remains.

XII.

Cooper Rose, in his travels, one day met with a strange hunter; he was a little meagre and vivacious man, whose sun-burnt figure and piercing eye denoted his hazardous profession. His manners were frank and bold. His eye shone under his peasant's hat; his powder-horn hung from a large black leathern belt, which also supported his bag net; he rode a small and very spirited horse, and was followed by nine dogs of different breeds.

The country which they had traversed was entirely wild, elephants alone had made the paths. Men came there for the first time, and it was to destroy.

They followed in silence the paths of the elephants, over the mountains and into the ravines. Cooper Rose, little used to march thus, began to find himself fatigued. "We shall soon be near the elephants," said the strange hunter, "and then we can sit down and watch them." They marched thus for a part of the day, when the guide, looking towards a small hill a long way off, announced that a herd of elephants was there feeding. The company took courage, and with new vigour set off on their march. A straight path conducted them very near to the place where the animals were feeding. The guide stopped; the hunter gave to his companions some lighted torches, and assigned to them the places where they should set fire to the bushes and the grass, in order to insure their retreat if by chance the elephants should show fight. They were browsing in full security, flapping their cheeks with their large ears, and enjoying their pasture with soft indolence. At the moment shots were heard, and an elephant fell, the herd had taken flight; they ran with the rapidity of which they are capable, upsetting every obstacle, breaking large trees like young shrubs. The following day they discovered nine or ten. The bushes prevented their being distinctly seen, but they heard them browsing. Guns were fired, and a fearful noise announced the flight of the animals, of which three fell mortally wounded. They were small, the largest not being more than three feet high. Roso made the observation that, considering the frequency of the tracks which they had met with, the country ought

HERD OF ELEPHANTS.   [Page 188.

to abound with elephants. The hunter told him that he was not deceived; that three years before he had met with more than three thousand on the banks of the river, but that since that time an immense number had been destroyed.

Our traveller, who delighted in this life of adventure, was astonished to hear the hunter express how much he desired to quit this wandering existence, and to establish himself quietly on his farm.

"I should have thought," said Rose to him, "that a peaceable life would appear very monotonous to you after so many daily emotions." "No, truly," replied the hunter; "I have a wife and little children, and I have been constrained to do this by necessity and by the debts which I have to pay: soon all these difficulties will be surmounted. In the space of twenty months I have killed eight hundred elephants. Four hundred have been brought down by the good gun which I still carry, but it will be with great pleasure that I shall cease to make use of it. How could I count the number of times when the elephants, seeking to take vengeance on me, have found themselves within a step of the place where I was crouching? One day I had just fired into a numerous group; the sound was repeated by the echo and deceived the elephants, which flying in the opposite direction, passed into the bush where my Hottentots and I were concealed The most intrepid hunter succumbs at last. Not long since, pursued by a rhinoceros, I was about to leap down a precipice, of the depth of which I was ignorant. No, sir, this life of dangers is not desirable. Would you believe that one day, not having any food, I was obliged to eat the leather of my shoes?"

CHAPTER XIII.

The Elephant (*continued.*)

The Royal Elephant Hunt at the Knysna.

[As an appropriate conclusion, we have ventured to quote from *The Times*' correspondent the last recorded elephant hunt in which H.R.H. the Duke of Edinburgh performed the most prominent part.—TRANSLATOR.]

As soon as it had become known that His Royal Highness had arrived in Simon's Bay, all the principal places of the colony became anxious to receive a visit from him. In a happy hour the people of the Knysna also sent him an invitation, and, as an inducement to him to accept it, promised, if he came, to provide him with amusement after their own fashion. In every quarter the Duke can find grand dinners and grand balls and suppers; but a dance on the green sward, with an elephant for a partner, is what but few places in the world can afford. Therefore, in the afternoon of Saturday the 7th of September, His Royal Highness, accompanied by the Governor and some other gentle-men, went on board the war-vessel *Racoon*, in Simon's

Bay, and steamed down the coast, arriving off the Knysna Heads on Monday morning. As the *Racoon* draws too much water to permit her to cross the bar, the Duke and his companions transhipped themselves to the *Petrel*, which entered the river at noon. That morning great numbers had come in from the country, so that the place was crowded with people. About one o'clock the Duke landed, and was received on the jetty by the authorities. He then mounted a horse, and with a large escort, amid cheering and firing of guns, rode into the village, which was handsomely decorated with flags and arches. At one of these the usual loyal address was presented, and then the Duke and his companions retired to the house that had been prepared for their accommodation. That night the village was illuminated, and bonfires blazed on the surrounding hills, for the people of the Knysna felt proud and honoured by the Duke's visit, and did everything in their power to give him a suitable reception.

The next morning, Tuesday the 10th of September, was very fine at the Knysna, and shortly after sunrise a goodly cavalcade of some forty horsemen, with His Royal Highness at their head, and attended by seven bullock-waggons, started for elephant shooting at Middle Erf, which is about a good hour's ride from the village. There one of the scouts met us with the information that the old bull elephant, which the Duke was desirous of shooting, had left that quarter only the night before. They had that morning traced him from his usual haunts into the great forest, so there was nothing for it but to rightabout face, and, with left shoulders forward, we abandoned the road we had come and dashed across the country. In less than an hour we came again on the new road at the entrance to the forest, where, as soon as the waggons arrived, we camped near a pretty stream and had breakfast. At this place we remained about an hour, and then proceeded for ten miles, with the forest bordering the road all the way on either hand. Forest, forest, far as the eye could reach, nothing but forest. It was really a fine ride, and afforded very great enjoyment to all the party not accustomed to such scenery. Then we arrived at the former convict station, called Yzen Nek, where there is now a road-side hotel, at which we halted and got some forage for our horses. After a considerable delay we started again, leaving the forest behind us, only patches of it being seen in the ravines here and there as we rode along. It is about four miles from Yzen Nek to Buffel's Nek, which is a very elevated site, and from which there is a splendid view of mountain scenery. Arrived at Buffel's Nek and the waggons having come up, the camp was pitched, and "all went merry as a

o

marriage bell," but unfortunately, about nine o'clock, it began to rain heavily, accompanied with a strong wind. All who were under canvas made it out pretty well, but those who had to rough it, with mother earth for a bed and little beside the canopy of heaven for a blanket, had a hard time of it. Some crept under the waggons, in the hope of finding that shelter which they sought in vain, while others sat cowering over the fires, shivering from the cold and wishing for daylight, with nothing but a blanket or an extra coat thrown over their shoulders to protect them from the pelting storm. The poor horses, too, suffered a good deal, for they were tied up at sunset in the open air, and with but a very scanty allowance of forage to appease their hunger. But a stormy night, like every other trouble, must come to an end at last, and at the very first peep of early dawn the camp was astir. All were in good spirits, notwithstanding the discomfort many of us had undergone; but the rain still continued at intervals, and therefore it was past noon before the horses were saddled and we made a start. After riding for more than an hour along a high ridge, one of the scouts came up to say that eleven elephants were grazing in the valley at a short distance, and on advancing a little farther we saw them very distinctly. A messenger was now sent back to the Governor, who was a considerable way behind, to tell him to hasten up, for the Duke was anxious that his Excellency should enjoy the sight, and certainly it was a sight in every way worth enjoying.

There we sat, high up on the ridge, with the valley below us, in which the elephants were quietly grazing and little dreaming that enemies were near, while on the further side of the valley the scenery was splendid, mountain upon mountain, in every conceivable shape, stretching away before us to the verge of the horizon. It was truly a noble prospect, and no doubt Mr. Brierley, the Duke's artist, will do it justice. The Governor having come up, and a considerable time having been spent in watching the elephants, the Duke made a move, and, followed by the hunters, descended into the valley. Here the party separated, the Duke, escorted by a few specially selected men, under the command of Mr. George Rex, taking the direction which was considered most likely to bring him near the elephants, while the others placed themselves in such spots as they thought would enable them also to get a shot. But things did not turn out according to our wishes, for, after spending more than an hour in vain attempts to find the elephants, which were now hidden from view by the bush, the Duke did not obtain a sight of them until they had got to the further side of a broad and deep ravine, and he was therefore compelled to fire at a long range.

He discharged six shots, all of which took effect, and then the others also blazed away; but though three elephants were wounded, and two of them very severely, they managed to effect their escape. It was thought, however, that they were not far off, and therefore young Atkinson, who was one of the Duke's personal escort, entered the bush alone, which was a service of no little danger, to ascertain if they were to be found; but it was all to no purpose, and so, as it was then getting dark, there was nothing for it but to retrace our steps to the camp. As we continued to wend our way back, we found the vast difference between the same path by day and the same path by night. In the morning, when we were fresh for the work before us, and elated with the prospect of a good day's sport, we thought nothing of the rugged hillside track, with its ups and downs, and fords and swamps, but the same track proved very miserable when we were hungry, weary, and exhausted. All, too, felt disappointment more or less, because things had not turned out according to our hopes; but, notwithstanding that, the Duke was greatly pleased. He had seen the elephants, and proved himself to be a crack shot, and he declared that, if nothing more was to come of his hunting, he would still derive the highest gratification from his visit. That night there was a little rain and a cold cutting wind, but nothing like what there was the night before, so those who had to rough it in the open air managed to get some repose. The camp, as usual, was astir at peep of day next morning, and the scouts and hunters made a start to look for the elephants that had been wounded the day before, but the Duke did not join their party. He kept about the camp, merely going a short distance alone with a light gun to get a shot at small birds. The others who did not accompany the hunters amused themselves as they best could. The Governor wrote letters, Mr. Brierly made some sketches, and the officers of the *Petrel* (with the exception of Captain Gordon, who had gone after the elephants) took their guns and crossed to the opposite hill to try and shoot bucks; but on the whole, some of us that day found it rather slow work. In the evening the scouts and hunters returned without having seen anything of the elephants, and therefore the Duke, whose time was limited, as he had arranged to leave the Knysna on Saturday, determined to return to Middle Erf in the morning, and make another attempt to shoot the old bull. That night there was no rain, but we had a repetition of a strong, cold, and biting blast, only it was from another quarter; and, indeed, Buffel's Nek is so elevated and exposed to the west and east that I much doubt whether it would be possible to find any night in the year there without the same annoyance. The next morning there was a new arrival in the camp, who had ridden through from the Knysna during the night to inform the Duke that some of the scouts had seen the elephants the previous evening on the edge of a detached piece of forest, which is situated on Middle Erf. This news confirmed the Duke in his determination to leave Buffel's Nek, and it was therefore yet very early when word was passed along to saddle up and mount. Prior to starting we had nothing but coffee, for we expected to make a halt at the other side of the forest, and have something to eat on the same spot where we had previously breakfasted. That hope, however, we were not destined to realize, for we were still a couple of miles from where we proposed to saddle off, when a scout came galloping up to let the Duke know that it was hardly an hour since he had seen the elephants at Middle Erf. Of course there was then an end of all thoughts of breakfast, necessary though it was—for who would delay for such a purpose with, it might be said, the game in view? On, therefore, we dashed; but, prior to entering on the final act of the drama, permit me to say a few words descriptive of the site of the Duke's exploit. Middle Erf forest, then, which will be famous in the annals of the Knysna for all time to come, crowns the summit of a gentle hill, within two hundred yards of the public road leading to Plettenberg's Bay. It is not more than a mile in circumference, and stands completely detached from the great forest, which is about six hundred yards distant at the nearest point.   It is admirably situated for holding an elephant at bay; and, in fact, if the Duke had had the choice of every part of the colony, he could not have selected a spot better adapted for his purpose.   As soon as we reached Middle Erf, straps were put on the dogs, and they were held fast; for the Duke intended to stalk the elephants if he should still find them in the open country; but on reconnoitering he could see nothing of them, and therefore the dogs were turned loose again, while most of the hunters were directed to go to the rear of the detached piece of forest and drive the elephants out of the north side, where the Duke and his personal escort were stationed.   Presently one elephant showed himself at the Duke's side, trumpeting and fighting with the dogs.   This elephant disappeared and came in view again half-a-dozen times, on two of which he raised his head and held up his trunk perpendicularly, as if trying to discover by that means what chance he had of making his escape.   He evidently wanted to break covert, but hesitated to do so from seeing the Duke and his party, who had stationed themselves directly across the path usually taken by the elephants in passing from Middle Erf to the great forest.   The Duke had been hitherto standing about three hundred yards from the edge of the detached piece of forest, but he and his escort now decided to advance within close range and fire at the elephant the next time he made his appearance. An advance was accordingly made by the party, but, to their surprise, no elephant or dogs were then to be seen. All had become suddenly quiet at that side, and it was very evident, from the direction in which their barking was heard, that the dogs had gone towards the rear. The fact is, there were three elephants afoot, and the particular one which had appeared repeatedly to the Duke and his party had managed to elude the dogs and conceal himself from view. Mr. George Rex, the captain of the hunt, now called to a boy at a little distance, and told him to mount his horse and ride to ascertain what was going on in the rear. It is right, however, here to remark that Middle Erf is intersected by a narrow road, each side of which is thickly overgrown with fine bush. Along this road the boy had to proceed, but he had not gone far into the fine bush when we saw him returning at full speed with the elephant after him in hot pursuit. The monster, which has great speed when he chooses to use it, was evidently gaining on the horse, while the boy, calling out in Dutch, " Fire, fire ! for God's sake fire, or I shall be killed !" rode for protection towards the Duke's party, and galloped round their flank. Upon that the elephant did not slacken his pace, but with ears and tail erect he rushed on right in the direction of the Duke, who was standing in the centre of his line. There was something very peculiar in the way the elephant advanced. It did not look like either a trot or a gallop, but more resembled the gliding motion of a ship in smooth water, as if the immense monster were bearing down under a press of sail before the wind. It has been put into the Cape papers that the Duke went on his knee to fire, but nothing of the kind occurred. He coolly took his large gun from the hand of young Atkinson, who had been carrying it for him, and did not pull a trigger until the elephant was within less than twenty yards. He then discharged both barrels in quick succession, sending one bullet into the animal's head just above the right eye, and then hitting him with the second bullet a little lower down, between the trunk and the root of the right tusk. No one could possibly have been more steady and deliberate than the Duke was when he fired, and it was fortunate for himself that he was able to display such pluck; for he allowed the elephant to get so close, that if he had been at all nervous, and his aim less sure, his own life and the lives of some of those at his side would inevitably have been sacrificed. As soon as the elephant received the Duke's two bullets he stopped in his career, shook his head, and reeled round, presenting his broadside; he then staggered a few yards further, and when he was in the act of falling, some of the others fired; but these shots were superfluous, for the Duke had given the poor brute his *quietus*, and he would have died on the spot if not a second gun had been discharged. On either hand of the Duke on this occasion stood the five good men and true who were his personal escort throughout the whole hunt—Messrs. G. and T. Rex, A. H. and J. Duthie, and G. R. Atkinson. Besides these there were on the spot Sir W. Currie, General Bisset, Captain Gordon of the *Petrel*, and Captain Taylor. The Duke's own man, Smith—his *fidus Achates*, who is always near his master—was also present. The Governor and some others, who had been watching what took place from a hill at a little distance, now galloped up, and every one congratulated the Duke on his success. His escort then assisted him to get on the top of the elephant, where he stood, while all gave three lusty cheers, which were taken up by the hunters at the rear. The Duke then took off his jacket, and began skinning the elephant, in which all present joined. Meantime the officers of the *Petrel* and some others went to the rear, where the hunters had got a second elephant at bay, which was despatched after receiving not less than forty shots. Around this second elephant, after the first one had been skinned, the Duke, who had the necessary apparatus with him, placed his personal escort, and took a photograph of the group, which, it is to be regretted, was afterwards found to be a failure. He then sat upon the elephant, with Mr. G. Rex beside him, and they had their photographs taken, but that did not turn out more successful. Before the elephants were skinned the Duke measured them both, and they were found to be just the same size—interesting twins, perhaps, who were wandering from forest to forest to complete their education. Their measurement was ten feet in height, twenty-four feet from the tip of the trunk to the tip of the tail, and seventeen feet round the body. Whatever one may think of the elephant when ranging at large in his native wilds—and he is then certainly a noble-looking object—there can be no more ugly animal when dead; but his flesh, if he is in condition, is good eating, as I can testify from experience.

The Duke passed that night a short distance from Middle Erf, where the camp had been pitched, and the next morning rode into the village before noon, escorted by the hunters and a number of other horsemen. Shortly afterwards the waggons came in with the heads and skins of the elephants, and the whole place crowded round to have a sight. The

Duke walked about highly elated, and evidently pleased that his trophies attracted so much notice. About one o'clock he started to go on board the *Petrel*, a great many accompanying him to the jetty. Here he took a warm farewell of those with whom he had become personally acquainted. As he shook hands with the Messrs. Rex, Duthies, and G. R. Atkinson, he thanked them in the kindest manner for having exerted themselves so much to render his hunt successful. He then got into the boat and was pulled off to the *Petrel*, which in about an hour afterwards steamed out to sea, amid the mingled cheers and regrets of all the inhabitants of the Knysna.

Before leaving the village the Duke gave a liberal gratuity to each of the scouts, and after his arrival in Cape Town he forwarded presents to those who had been his personal escort. To one of them, who acted as captain of the hunt, he sent a handsome gold watch, and the others received valuable rings, which they will always highly prize on account of the donor.

CHAPTER XIV.

The Ostrich.

I.

A VOLUMINOUS massive body mounted on tall legs of
four feet or more, and carrying a neck as long as
its legs; a very small head and very large feet;
great floating feathers; a tail in the form of a plume—
such are, in the physiognomy of the ostrich, the traits
which, even at a distance, the least attentive look
embraces.

Approaching nearer, one sees that the head is bald
and flat; the eye large and bright; the beak short,
blunt, and depressed; the neck slender, covered with
grey down; that the feathers which cover the body
are large, soft, half curled, and glossy, of a magnificent colour and brilliancy in the male; the wings
themselves, composed of feathers with flexible stems,
are out of all proportion with the dimensions of the
animal: they evidently cannot serve them for flying,
and they seem to be there only as a kind of apology.
If we examine one of these feathers, we discover, in

fact, that the barbules do not adhere together, as is the case with almost all other birds.

No sooner does the ostrich begin to walk, than we are struck with the suppleness of his body; his long neck balances itself gracefully, his trunk takes a kind of pitching motion, his stumps of wings open as if to catch the wind; and the ease of his march, the elasticity of his step, the extent and quickness of his strides, soon teach us that he is as generously endowed as a terrestrial, as he is deprived as an aërial animal. Besides, every one knows that the ostrich is one of the swiftest pedestrians that exist, perhaps *the* swiftest, for if, when he is hunted, he had sense enough to direct his flight in a straight line. the best horse would be incapable of running him down.

II.

One can understand that such a singular animal has given rise to many fables. " There is scarcely any subject of natural history about which more absurdities have been spoken," writes Buffon. The Arabs believe the ostrich to be the issue of a camel and a bird; Suidas gave him the neck and feet of a donkey; G. Warren made an aquatic bird of him; others assure us that he never drinks. Léon L'Africain refuses him the sense of hearing. It has been said that he feeds principally on stones, wood, and iron. Aldrovando represents him enjoying a horse-shoe; it has even been pretended that he would swallow red-hot coals. Marmol, in his "Description de l'Afrique," says that he digests red-hot iron. "I would not deny," writes Buffon, "that they might sometimes even swallow red-hot iron, provided it was in very small quantities, but I do not think that even that could be done with impunity." They have been called the worst of mothers: *Struthio dura est in pullos suos quasi non sint sui.*

They have been denied all intelligence, even to the extent of being too stupid to seek their safety by flight; "and," says Belon, "if by chance it finds a bush, they say that it is such a foolish bird, that in hiding its head therein it imagines its whole body to be safe." Belon had taken that from Pliny; Kolbe repeats it in his "Description du Cap de Bonne Espérance." A stone extracted from its stomach procures good digestion to him who hangs it round his neck. But enough of fiction; let us now go to facts.

III.

THE ostrich has the sense of sight very fully developed. It can see, it is said, six miles. It hears equally well, and can never be approached except by surprise.

It is quite otherwise with its sense of taste ; and the want of nicety in this sense, joined to the voracity and to the instinct common among birds, which leads it to introduce hard substances into its stomach, to augment the strength of trituration of that organ, causes it, in captivity at least, to swallow without discernment all objects, whatever they may be, which are presented to it, or which come within reach of its beak. Wood, bone, stones, metals, glass, paper, pieces of money, nails—all are good for it. As soon as it is seized, the object is forced down the throat by a backward movement.

M. Henri Aucapitaine reports that the *Bureau des Affaires Publiques*, at Cherchell, possessed an ostrich penned in one of the interior courts. "Every evening," says he, "we amused ourselves by feeding him with old papers, envelopes, and pieces of newspapers, which he swallowed greedily, and with evident gusto."

The traveller Richardson saw an ostrich in an African village, where it wandered about in full liberty, gathering up everything, like a ragman.

MM. Verreaux relate, that at the Cape, one of the ostriches which they possessed swallowed, one after the other, a large piece of soap and a copper candlestick, which latter was some time afterwards ejected quite flattened.

Ostriches were being exhibited at St. Quentin. One gentleman, on whose breast shone a beautiful gold chain, having approached within reach of the beak of one of these birds, saw, in the twinkling of an eye, his chain and watch pass from the neck and pocket of their proprietor, into the stomach of the gluttonous animal.

An ostrich preserved in the Museum of Natural History had in its body, when it died, about a pound of stones, pieces of iron and copper, and half-worn coins. Vallisnieri dissected one of these animals, and here is the inventory of the objects which he found there : cords, stones, glass, iron, copper, pewter, and above all a lump of lead, the last thing swallowed, and which did not weigh less than a pound. One individual, opened by Perrault, had swallowed seventy pieces of copper money, already reduced to three-fourths by their sojourn in the robust organ which contained them. Perrault attributed their wear to a mechanical action. Vallisnieri, on the contrary, without excluding the action of friction, saw there also a particular chemical action. This is the true opinion. Cuvier confirms it in these words :— " The bits of iron found in the stomach "—speaking of an ostrich which had lived in a menagerie—" were not only worn as they would have been by trituration with other hard bodies, but they had evidently been corroded by some juice, which could be seen above all by the inequality of the chinks which had been produced. The fragments of nails presented all the appearance of true corrosion."

Most frequently these errors of *régime* have no serious inconvenience. One ostrich had a nail implanted in the inner sides of the gizzard; another had two nails lodged in the thick part of the mesentery (where they could only have reached by perforating the stomach), and they had caused a very hard greenish concretion, with which they were entirely coated. Neither of these animals appeared in the least unwell. But it often happens to those in captivity to become the victims of their avidity. One ostrich is mentioned which died from having swallowed a large quantity of quick-lime. The menagerie of Paris possessed, twelve years since, a magnificent couple, which it was hoped would breed; but a stone having fallen on the glass roof of the den, the male and female hastened to swallow the broken glass, which lacerated their entrails. In the same establishment an ostrich succumbed, after thirty-four days, to an attack of indigestion, caused by a dose of a pound and a half of nails. Dr. Berg mentions one which was killed by swallowing an enormous shop-key.

IV.

GRASS is their favourite nourishment, as well in the wild state as in captivity; but to the aromatic and salty vegetation of the desert they constantly add molluscs, insects, and reptiles. A report addressed by Laghouat to the *Société d'Acclimatation* states that they eat rats, jerboas, serpents, lizards, and slugs; he adds, that they are very fond of grasshoppers at the Cape. The ostriches bred by the farmers sometimes swallow the chickens. M. Aucapitaine reports that molluscs formed the favourite food of the ostrich before referred to.

The Arabs say that the ostrich kills the viper with a blow of its beak, and eats it. It eats also serpents, insects, grasshoppers, scorpions, lizards, large fruits called *hadj*, abounding in the desert, and proceeding from a creeping plant, bitter as turpentine, with leaves like those of the water-melon. As soon as they come out of the egg the young ostriches begin to seek insects and small reptiles, and it appears that they feed themselves exclusively.

It is agreed that ostriches support long fasts, which must be the case, for the desert can only have for its inhabitants beings inured to all privations; but it is not so well agreed as to the limit of time during which they can remain without food. It would seem probable that the limit varies according to times and places (it must not be forgotten that the ostrich is nomadic), and also whether the animal is free, tame, or captive.

If we examine the reports sent to the Zoological Society from different parts of Africa, and collected with talent by M. Gosse, of Geneva, we are at first struck by seeing these reports differing often in the most notable manner on almost all points. As to the *régime* of the ostrich, its character, its conjugal manners, the construction of its nest; of the period of laying, the number of eggs, their arrangement, the duration and the circumstances of incubation; the numeric proportion of the sexes; of the manner in which the ostrich is affected by the changes of time, or of the duration of its life, these reports are quite contradictory of each other. But most frequently the contradiction is but apparent; and on a little reflection one is convinced that, apart from some badly observed facts and some individual cases maladroitly generalized, the numerous divergences of the reports simply attest changes to which, in order to accommodate itself to the variations of time and place, the ostrich in its peregrinations is constrained to conform its habits; so that, in fact, far from contradicting, these reports really agree with each other. It is simply this, that the habits of a wandering species have not in all their details an absolutely fixed character. A crowd of special cases depart from the rule, this departure being confined within certain limits, at least for long periods of time. In a word, in this matter our formulas have but the value of means.

Ostriches support thirst perfectly, but nothing is more false than to say that they never drink.

The Arabs say that they drink a little every day when there is any water to be had. Messieurs Verreaux have seen them drinking in the Elephant River.

General Daumas reports that he has known them make many days' journey in search of water. It is said that those which have been deprived of water for a long time show extraordinary joy at the approach of a storm. They are then seen running about in every direction, with their wings extended, turning themselves about, and at last rushing off in the direction of the lightning.

They bathe, always taking care to choose water sufficiently shallow, so that when they sit down their heads may still be above water; but they cannot swim. An English traveller in South Africa, Mr. Gordon Cumming, says that they are exceedingly fond of salt. Barley is the food which those seem to prefer which the Arabs do not send out into the pasture fields.

V.

THE muscular strength of the ostrich is extraordinary. "In the desert," says M. Daumas, "it has no other enemy to fear but man. It resists the dog, the jackal, the hyæna, and the eagle : man alone triumphs over it."

Livingstone remarks that he saw one, pursued by dogs, break the spine of the one nearest to it with a blow of .its foot. M. Edouard Verreaux saw a negro die from a blow received in the stomach from the foot of an ostrich. An Arab hunter, of whom more presently, narrowly escaped a similar fate.

No better idea of its strength can be given than the fact of its having been employed for riding from the remotest period. Mounted ostriches figured in the Roman circus.

A certain tyrant of Egypt, named Firmin, employed them for his use ; and the natives of Africa often do the same.

"One sees at the Cape," says Sparrman, "in the Government menagerie, several tame ostriches. These easily allow themselves to be mounted by those who wish to make the attempt."

We read that an English traveller, Mr. Moore, encountered in the Sahara an Arab mounted on an

ostrich crossing the desert. He took the bird to
Fatatenda, whence M. Connor sent him to the
Governor of Jamesfort, on the Gambia.

Examples are abundant. We will only stop to
relate that cited by Adanson, the truth of which is
above suspicion.

"The same day two ostriches, which had been
kept for about two years in this district (Podor),
gave me a spectacle which is too rare not to merit
being reported.

"These gigantic birds, which I had never seen
except in the burning and sandy country on the
left of the Niger, I saw there at my ease. Though
still young, these ostriches almost equalled in size
the largest. They were so tame that two little
negroes mounted together the larger of the two;
this one no sooner felt their weight than it started
off full speed, and carried them several times round
the village; and it seemed only possible to stop it
by barring the passage. This trial pleased me so
much that I wished to have it repeated; and in
order to try their strength I mounted a full-grown
negro on the smallest, and two others on the largest.
This load did not seem disproportioned to their
vigour. At first they started off at a cautious canter,
but presently, when they had got excited, they
spread their wings, as if to catch the wind, and went

off at such a speed that they seemed scarcely to touch the ground.

"Every one has seen a partridge running, and knows that no man is capable of catching it; and it is not difficult to imagine that if it had a greater stride its speed would be considerably augmented.

"The ostrich runs like the partridge, and I am persuaded that they could leave far behind them the swiftest English horse that could be put in pursuit of them. It is true they could not keep up as long a race as the horses, but undoubtedly they would accomplish a short one more quickly. I have been many times witness of this spectacle, which should give some idea of the prodigious strength of the ostrich, and the use which could be made of it if means could be found of mastering and instructing it as horses are taught."

The largest of these two ostriches must then have carried upwards of 300 pounds weight without apparent inconvenience.

M. Edouard Verreaux relates, on the contrary, that having mounted a captive ostrich in a shed, the bird had the greatest difficulty in carrying him. But this experience by no means invalidates contrary testimony. M. Gosse makes the reasonable observation that this faculty which the ostrich possesses of carrying weights so disproportioned to the size of its body, is doubtless due to a physiological phenomenon, which is common to birds which rise into the air, viz., that not only are the greater part of its bones vacuous, and in direct communication with the lungs, but the bird can also at will fill with warm air many membranous reservoirs, which are found near the wings, under the stomach, and around the thighs—veritable air balloons, which lighten the weight borne by the legs. When it is not racing or otherwise excited, these sacks are not inflated, and consequently the ostrich cannot support so considerable a weight.

———

VI.

THE speed of the animal does not yield to its strength. Cuvier says that it surpasses that of all known animals. "It is such," adds he, "that those who mount the ostrich without having become accustomed to it, are soon suffocated, not being able to get their breath." This nearly happened to an inhabitant of Paris, M. Notré, who being at Marseilles in the year 1819, then weighing 140lbs., mounted a male Egyptian ostrich of large size. It took him such an astounding race, that he contemplates it even to this day with affright. Happily, he clung tightly round the neck of the bird, which at last stopped in some brushwood. Adanson says that the two ostriches of which we have before spoken, although they had not attained all the strength which age and liberty would have given them, and although laden with a considerable weight, "would have left far behind them the swiftest English horse that could have been sent in pursuit of them."

"I have seen them," says Sparrman, "sometimes within two gun-shots of me, and I have started in pursuit, but always without success."

Xenophon relates that the cavaliers of Cyrus were not more happy. Livingstone says that one can no more distinguish the legs of an ostrich when at its full speed, than one can see the spokes of the wheels of a carriage driven at full gallop; and he estimates that the bird can make twenty-seven miles an hour.

VII.

THE ostrich shines less in point of intelligence; but it by no means merits the reputation for stupidity which authors vie with each other in making for it. It is a gentle bird, gay, pacific, vigilant, eminently sociable, and not wanting, whatever may be said, in any of the family instincts.

Cumming one day surprised a flock of twelve

THE OSTRICH THEN TURNED ITS BLOWS AGAINST SI-MOHAMMED.

[*Page* 219.

ostriches, which were no larger than guineafowls. "The mother," says he, "sought to deceive us after the manner of the wild duck. She started off, extending her wings, then let herself fall to the ground as though she were wounded; whilst the male cunningly departed with the little ones in an opposite direction."

Livingstone frequently mentions young coveys going under the conduct of a male, which endeavoured to appear lame, in order to turn upon himself the attention of the hunters.

We read in the *Chevaux du Sahara* that when the hunters catch up the young ones, in sight of the male, he becomes excessively agitated and manifests the most vivid grief ; but he does not give himself up to moaning. He is not wanting in courage.

Here is an instance which proves it. It is related in a report, addressed from Géryville to the Zoological Society (Paris). "Si-Djelloul-Ben-Hamza, and his brother Si-Mohammed-Ben-Hamza, one day, whilst hunting the ostrich, came upon the track of a whole family, conducted by one male and two females. Si-Mohammed, having come first in sight of the ostriches, fired and wounded one of the females. The male then rushed at him, and struck the horse on the chest with his leg, on which the latter threw his rider and fled. The ostrich then turned its blows against Si-Mohammed, and only left him, deprived of consciousness, on seeing Si-Djelloul coming to the assistance of his brother."

"Whilst riding out one morning," says Thunberg, who was then at the Cape, "I passed near to a female ostrich, which was brooding; she rose, and started in pursuit of me, in order to prevent my seeing her eggs, or young ones. As soon as I turned my horse's head round she fled, but when I continued my journey she commenced again to pursue me."

The excessive timidity with which they are reproached is but the result of the incessant hunting to which they are subjected. Those kept in captivity are not in the slightest degree timid, nor are those which have no knowledge of man.

Richardson relates, that having reached the plateau of Hamala, where the ostriches have not been disturbed, he had the grand sight of a flock of eleven of these birds feeding tranquilly like sheep, without showing any disposition to fly.

I have said that they are very sociable. A flock of from two to three hundred has occasionally been met with in the desert, mingling with giraffes, cougas, zebras, and antelopes. This sociability renders it an easy matter to tame them.

"Young ostriches are easily tamed," says General Daumas; "they play with the children, and sleep in the tent. When removing, they follow the camels; there is no example of one of these thus trained ever taking flight. They are very gay, they frolic with the horsemen, dogs, &c. Should a hare start up, all the people are off in pursuit; and the ostrich becomes excited, and takes part in the chase. When it meets a child having any food in its hand, it quietly throws the child on the ground, and tries to take away whatever it was carrying. The ostrich is a great thief, or rather it wants to swallow whatever it sees. The Arabs are very watchful of it when they are counting their money. It would soon cause the disappearance of a few dollars."

It is by no means rare to see a tired child, at a short distance from the *douar*, placed on the back of an ostrich, which with its little load directs its steps straight to the tent, the little cavalier holding on by the feathers. On journeys, when it is wished to prevent its running to right or left, a cord is passed round its legs, and it is held by another cord attached to this one.

In the Senaar country, they are bred in the same way as poultry is bred elsewhere.

According to Dr. Berg, in many black villages on the banks of the Senegal, and in most of the camps of the Maures, on the right bank of the river, one ostrich at least is counted among their indispensables. These birds are not intended as objects of commerce; they never kill them; they form, in fact, part of the tribe, or of the village.

Sometimes they are hatched in the tent by artificial means.

As soon as they are six months old, no further trouble is taken with them, and they go to seek nourishment in the neighbouring pastures, taking care, however, always to find themselves close to the tent at meal times. The farmers in the neighbourhood of the Cape allow them to feed in their fields, and they never attempt to fly.

Amongst the *abiades* of the Sahara, flocks of twenty or thirty individuals follow the cattle to the pastures, and return with them every evening. One traveller saw at Esne some ostriches belonging to the Governor promenading freely in the town, visiting the markets and returning to the palace in the evening.

This attachment and obedience is obtained by treating the ostrich with kindness. It is necessary to caress them often when they are young, to be careful not to frighten them, and never to be sharp with them. It has been stated that ostriches which have been given away and taken a very long distance from their domicile, have returned to their first master.

"I find them," says M. Bouteille, director of the Zoological Gardens at Grenoble, "more susceptible of attachment than most of our domestic animals. They allow themselves to be touched and caressed by the persons who have the care of them, and they appear quite sensible of the pleasure. I can take our young ostriches into my hands and carry them away, without the parents making the least hostile demonstration, whilst the sight alone of a strange man or animal is sufficient to put them in a fury; then they set up their feathers and lower their heads, like hens defending their brood."

CHAPTER XV.

The Ostrich (*continued*).

VIII.

DURING the period of laying, this pacific humour, with the male at least, gives place to a violent character. The males are then said to exhibit such rage that it is difficult to approach them; and sometimes even their masters have been obliged to defend themselves against them with stones, clubs, and even guns. North of the equator the laying season begins towards the end of autumn, and continues until spring. Its period and duration depend on the degree of fertility of the year; but in any case it takes up a large share of the life of an ostrich. The Arabs say even that if food is abundant this troubled period is prolonged through a great portion of the year. It is then that the male takes that roseate tint on his legs and neck, which is caused by the activity acquired by circulation; he puts himself in pursuit of the female, and closing his beak and drawing up his neck, the top of which is prodigiously dilated, he gives utterance to repeated hoarse guttural cries, which so much resemble the roaring of a lion, though more feeble, that the Hottentots are sometimes deceived; and one of the *employés* of the menagerie of Paris mistook it many times in the night. Mr. Hardy confirms this fact. The female flies before the male. The pursuit continues four or five days, during which the male neither eats nor drinks. The female does not separate from the male, and only quits him when the education of the family is completed.

IX.

Both sexes take part in making the nest; some say that the nest is built on flat ground, and in open places, others on ground a little elevated and surrounded. These differences evidently arise out o local conditions.

The nest is dug out of the sand by the beak; the thrown-out sand is disposed all round, forming a projecting rim; on the outside a trench is dug for carrying off the water. Laying is rapid or slow, according to the greater or less abundance of food, and even according to its quality. All the females of the same household lay their eggs in the same nest.

One female will lay from twenty-five to thirty eggs, each egg being equal in weight to about twenty-five hen-eggs. Besides the eggs sat upon, others are placed outside of the nest, often in little cavities dug out specially.

What is their destination? It is a discovery of M. Vaillant, to whom we owe the first exact ideas we have had as to the habits of the ostrich.

A female had got up about twenty yards from him: "Suspecting that it was a sitter, I hastened to reach the place from which she had risen, and I found eleven eggs, still warm, and four others dispersed at two or three feet from the nest. I called my companions, who came up at once. I broke one of the eggs, and found a young one already formed, the size of a chicken, ready to come out of its shell. I supposed all the eggs were rotten; my people thought very differently: each one hastened to fall on the nest; but Amiroo took possession of four others, desiring to give me a feast, and assuring me that I should find them excellent. It was then I learnt from this savage that which the Hottentots themselves are ignorant of, and which is not known to naturalists, since no one that I am aware of has spoken of it, and which I have had more than one opportunity of verifying, viz., that the ostrich always places within reach of the nest a certain number of eggs proportioned to those which she destines for incubation. These eggs not being sat upon are preserved fresh for a long time, and the provident instinct of the mother destines them for the first nourishment of those which are about to be hatched. Experience has convinced me of the truth of this assertion; and whenever I have found the nests of ostriches, many eggs have been found separated in this way."

The information of M. Vaillant is confirmed by that which Achmet, quartermaster of the spahis, related to M. Aucapitaine in 1856. "At the moment," says he, "when the young are hatched, the mother goes to seek one of the supernumerary eggs, breaks it, and makes the young ones partake of the nourishment." According to other natives, she conducts her young ones to the nutritious eggs, and makes them open them. The report sent from Géryville to the Zoological Society (Paris), asserts beyond this, that if the ostrich should break one of the eggs on which she is sitting, she replaces it by one of the outside eggs. Livingstone says that, according to the natives of South Africa, the supernumerary eggs are intended for the need of those first hatched, "in order that they may wait until the others are hatched, and that all may then go together to pasture elsewhere;" an explanation which has some appearance of truth, as the hatching takes place successively.

Incubation takes place day and night, or at night only, according to the degree of the circumambient temperature. The carcases of jackals, which are found in the neighbourhood, bear witness to the vigilance as well as to the strength of the male. The hatching of the young takes place successively, as we shall see. It is pretty generally agreed that the number of females is about double that of males. Their size at the time of hatching is about that of a small hen. It would appear that they continue with their parents until they are full grown.

X.

ÆLIAN relates that the ostrich is hunted in two ways :—

"The ostrich is taken by running down. It describes in its flight an exterior circle, whilst the hunters close up its route by following it in an interior circle, and thus, by tiring it out, they at last catch it.

"The following manœuvre is also employed in taking it. When it has been discovered by a clever man accustomed to this kind of chase, he fixes some very sharp-pointed spears round the nest, in a vertical position; the steel shines, and the hunter, retired to a distance, awaits in ambush the upshot of the event. Meanwhile the ostrich returns from her pasture full of tenderness for her young, and burning with the desire to rejoin them. At first she examines

here and there, and casts her looks all round for fear
that some one should observe her ; at last, overcome,
and yearning with maternal love, she spreads her
wings like a sail, and, carried away in a blundering
blind career, she rushes upon her nest, but—oh,
touching spectacle!—she encounters the spears, and
perishes, pierced through and through. The hunter
then comes up and takes the little ones with their
mother."

Let us now pass on to more positive facts. At
Khartoum, an old negro, who in his youth had been
one of the most intrepid buccaneers of the country,
thus described the hunt of the ostrich, as it is now
practised by the natives :—

" The ostrich is hunted on horseback, and the riders
are obliged to be accompanied by camels laden with
provisions. When one is discovered, they follow it
slowly without losing sight of it : the colossal bird
is not slow in leaving them far behind ; but having
reached a certain distance, as if to bid defiance to
the hunters, it stands and awaits them ; when they
are on the point of coming up with it, it starts off
on its rapid course, and then again waits for them.
The riders always follow it slowly. It is usually at
daybreak that the hunters commence the campaign,
and whilst the heat is not too much felt the ostrich
can, without danger, make parade of its superior

speed; nevertheless, these repeated races fatigue it insensibly, and when the sun becomes more powerful, the animal, which has already several times renewed the same plan, begins to exhibit signs of fatigue; and then the hunters, who have hitherto restrained their steeds, rush after it with full speed, and are not. long in exhausting and overcoming it. The first of the hunters that arrives within reach of it deals it a heavy blow with a club, and fells it to the ground. The riders leap from their horses, and one of them cuts the animal's neck, and puts its foot in the wound in order to prevent its plumes being soiled in the blood whilst it is fluttering about. When the bird has ceased to live they despoil it of its plumage, and if the horses and provisions permit, the chase is continued."

The same method appears to be in use at the Cape, as Sparrman relates:—"I have been told that a man mounted on the best horse could never reach the ostriches when they are off; but the hunter must nevertheless continue his chase, taking care to look after his horse, and prevent him from galloping too fast, whilst he can still perceive the bird from the summit of some hill. Then the ostrich, which has descended it running, cools down when it reaches the bottom, its joints stiffen, and it rarely fails, by at least the third race, in allowing itself to be taken, either alive or by a shot from the hunter's gun."

The Arabs of the Great Desert adopt a quite different plan. General Daumas has given us on this point, in the "Chevaux du Sahara," details full of interest, which he obtained from a professional hunter. We cannot do better than reproduce them, always abridging considerably.

There are in the desert two methods of hunting the ostrich : on horseback, and by watching.

"The real hunt is that on horseback. It is an excursion which lasts for seven or eight days. The most favourable period is that of great heat. A dozen hunters join together; each of them is accompanied by a servant, mounted on a camel, which carries water, barley for the horses, wheat flour, dates, a saucepan, and divers utensils. The horse has undergone for seven or eight days a special training. The rider has no other weapon than a club of wild olive or rosemary, from four to five feet long, and very heavy at one end.

"They start in the morning, and after one or two days' march, when they have arrived near the place where the ostriches have been signalled, and they begin to find traces of them, they stop and encamp. The next day two intelligent servants, entirely naked (with the exception of a handkerchief, used as drawers), are sent to reconnoitre. They carry a goat-skin full of water and a little bread, and they walk on until they discover the ostriches. As soon as they have perceived them, they lie down and watch them; then one of them remains, and the other goes to warn the company.

"The horsemen, guided by the man, proceed slowly towards the place where the ostriches are. Arrived at the last rising ground which can conceal them, they dismount. Two scouts creep forward to assure themselves that the birds are still in the same place. If these confirm the first informants, each one gives his horse a drink, but moderately, from the water carried on his camel's back. They deposit all the baggage on the spot where they had stopped, and without leaving any one in charge of it. Each horseman carries a goat-skin at his side. The servants and the camels follow in the tracks of the horses; each camel carries no more than the horse's barley supper, its own supper, and water for the men and animals.

"The hunters then separate and form a circle round the chase at a very great distance, and in such a manner as not to be perceived. The servants wait on the spot where their masters separated until they see them at their posts, then they march straight on: the ostriches fly in terror, but they encounter the horsemen, who at first only endeavour to drive them back into the circle. The ostriches thus begin to spend their strength in a rapid race, for as soon as they are surprised they do not husband their breath. They several times renew these manœuvres, always seeking to get out of the circle, and always returning, frightened by the horsemen. At the first signs of fatigue the hunters fall upon them. After some time the flock begins to disperse, and to show signs of weakness and lassitude by opening their wings; the horsemen then, certain of their prey, slacken their pace.

" Each one chooses an ostrich and follows it, and when he reaches it he deals it a heavy blow on the head, either from behind or the side, which fells it. The rider then dismounts in order to bleed it, taking care to hold the throat away from the body, so as not to soil the feathers. When the ostrich is on the point of being caught, it is so fatigued that, if the hunter does not wish to kill it, it is a very easy matter to bring it back quietly, directing it with the stick; it can then scarcely walk."

The ostrich is taken by watching for it when it has laid its eggs, that is about the middle of the month of November. Five or six hunters take with them two camels laden with provisions for a month at least, and begin by looking out for places where water has recently fallen. They are furnished on this occasion with guns and an abundant supply of ammunition. When they have discovered traces of the ostrich, the hunters examine them carefully; if they cross to and fro, and the grass is trampled under foot and not eaten, the bird has for certain made its nest in the neighbourhood.

In the morning, whilst the female is sitting, the hunters dig a hole on each side of the nest, and at twenty yards' distance, sufficiently deep to contain a man; they then cover it up with the long grass, so well known in the desert, in such a manner that the gun only shall appear: in these holes two of the best marksmen are lodged.

At the sight of this work the frightened female runs to rejoin the male, but he beats her and forces her to return to her nest. If these preparations were made whilst the male is sitting, he would go off in search of the female, and neither of them would be met with again.

They are careful not to disturb the returned female, the rule being to kill the male first; they therefore wait his return from pasture. Towards midday he arrives, and the hunter makes ready. The ostrich when sitting extends its wings in such a manner as to cover all the eggs; in this position it has bent up its extremely long legs under its thighs, a very favourable position for the marksman, who aims always in such a manner as to break the animal's legs, for if only wounded elsewhere it would still have a chance of making its escape. "Immediately the ostrich is struck down, they run up to it and bleed it. The marks of blood are covered over with sand, the body is carefully hidden."

At sunset the female returns: the absence of the male does not disquiet it; she believes it to be feeding, and sits on her nest. She is killed by the one of the two hunters who had not fired at the male.

They also shoot the ostrich when it goes to drink. The hunters simply make a hole near the water, and lie in ambush till the animal comes to quench its thirst.

The Arabs of the desert say of a good thing, that "it is like hunting the ostrich."

Bruce relates that the Arabs of Fazolp hunt the ostrich with dogs; they carry it off dead or alive, when the bird, which they have pursued without relaxation, falls from sheer exhaustion.

On the other extremity of Africa the bushmen have recourse to strategy.

They disguise themselves as ostriches. "This disguise," says a traveller, "is composed of a kind of saddle, the lower part of which is furnished with ostrich feathers in such a manner as to imitate the body of the bird, to which is added a head and neck of an ostrich stuffed with straw. '

"The hunter begins by painting his legs white; then he places the saddle of feathers on his shoulders, and holding with his right hand the lower part of the neck, in his left he carries his bow and poisoned arrows. 'I have seen,' says our author, 'the ostrich so perfectly imitated, that at a few yards' distance it was impossible to discover the fraud.'

"This human bird pretends to browse the grass, turns his head from side to side with an air of intelligence, shakes his feathers, walks and runs alternately, until he arrives within bow-shot of the flock; and when the ostriches take flight on seeing one of their number struck by an arrow, he flies with them. Sometimes the male ostriches give chase to this singular bird; then he manœuvres to avoid them, taking care that they shall not scent him, for from the moment he finds himself so placed as to cross their scent, the charm is broken; then it only remains for him to throw away his saddle and to fly with all speed, in order to avoid a wing blow, which would knock him down instantly."

CHAPTER XVI.

Crocodiles and Caymans.

I.—The Scene and the Actors.

THERE are three species or sub-species of crocodiles ; first, the *cayman*, also called the *alligator;* second, the *crocodile;* and third, the *gavial.*

The cayman, or alligator, may be thus recognized : when the mouth is closed the fourth tooth on each side of the lower jaw passes into a hole in·the upper jaw.

In the crocodile, in place of the hole just mentioned there is only an indentation, so that the fourth lower tooth remains visible when the mouth is closed.

. Lastly, in the gavial the upper jaw on each side is hollowed, not by a hole, as in the cayman, nor by one indentation, as with the crocodile, but with two indentations, in which the first and fourth lower teeth lodge. Moreover, the gavial has very straight and lengthy jaws, which form a kind of beak, more or less cylindrical.

Should you happen to encounter one of the crocodilian species on your journey, you are now in a position to determine at once to what species your friend belongs, whether he is a cayman, crocodile, or gavial.

The caymans belong to America, gavials to Asia, and crocodiles to America, Asia, Africa, and Oceanica.

All are inhabitants of hot regions, some even are found in the hot—almost boiling—mineral waters of Florida. The greater part live in the soft waters of rivers and lakes. A small number frequent the sea. Europe and Australia* are exempt.

II.—Numbers.

Count Forbin, in his "Voyage à Siam," says that he saw a great number in the neighbourhood of Bancok.

"The rivers of Java, both at their mouths and in the interior, are infested," says Thunberg ("Voyages en Japon"), "with crocodiles of a monstrous size. Often in my botanic excursions I saw them asleep in the sun."

---

* Alligators were found in the river Burdekin, North Australia, by McKinlay, some of which were nearly twenty feet long.—Translator.

CROCODILES ON THE MUD BANKS OF THE GUAYAQUIL.

[*Page* 239.

A recent account states that the rivers and lakes of Ceylon are stocked with crocodiles. Their hideous heads come out of the water ten or a dozen at a time. They are very common in Jamaica. La Condamine has seen a multitude of caymans from twelve to fifteen feet long, and even longer, in the Guayaquil; some stretched on the mud in the sun, others floating on the water like trunks of trees covered with a knotty desiccated bark. They abound in the Amazon, in the Oyapoc, in the Bay de Vincent Pinçon, and in the lakes of that region, to such an extent that, according to Lacépède, they impede by their multitude the navigation of the boats. M. de la Borde relates, that whilst running along the eastern shores of South America in a canoe, he encountered a dozen great caymans at the mouth of a little river which he wished to enter. As these animals were obstructing the passage, several shots were fired, in the hope of dispersing them. This was useless, and the narrator was obliged to wait for two hours before they thought proper to retire.

Let us pass now into Africa. The Dutch traveller Hamel ("Hist. Géne des Voyages") reports, that the rivers of the Corea are infested with crocodiles. Bosman, in his "Description de la Guinée," says that they are found in all the rivers of that country, and that he has seen as many as fifty in a day, and some of them twenty feet long. "The crocodile," writes M. de Golberry, in his "Fragments d'un Voyage en Afrique," "is found in all the rivers which empty into the sea between Cape Blanc and Cape de Palmes, and even in a great number of lagoons." Adanson has seen nearly two hundred at one time on the great Senegal river, floating together, which might easily be mistaken for the trunks of trees borne along by the stream.

M. du Chaillu thus describes a scene presented to him on the Anengué, a river of the Gaboon, at its junction with the Ogabay. "We then entered the Anengué. Its surface was covered with black mud banks, on which swarmed an incredible number o crocodiles. There were many hundreds of these disgusting monsters sunning themselves or wallowing in the mud, and diving to the bottom of the water in search of food. I have never seen a more hideous spectacle. Some of them were at least twenty feet long, and when they opened their horrible jaws, one might have said that they could have swallowed our little boats without any difficulty."

Livingstone has met with them in many of the rivers of South Africa. The quantity of them living on the Liambye is prodigious. "Every instant," he writes, "we see them sunning themselves on the sand-banks."

The traveller ascending the Nile does not encounter them until he reaches Upper Egypt. Mr. Combes ("Voyage en Egypte, en Nubie," &c.) reports, that the first he met with on his route was found above Syout. "I had but just embarked when they pointed out to me a crocodile stretched out in the sun. He was, as it were, embedded in the sand, and appeared to be asleep. Nevertheless, he lifted his head at our approach, and slipped slowly into the Nile." According to the people of the country, these animals do not pass below Said, because a venerable sheik had said, "You may come here, but you must not pass this barrier." But above this point they rapidly become very numerous, as may be judged by the following little picture, in the neighbourhood of Kéneh:—"Some of the palm trees in the neighbourhood of the town were bending under the weight of enormous crocodiles suspended from their branches, and swinging in the wind. The hunters, who had made a successful war on these formidable animals, had left them to dry in the sun, in order afterwards to offer them to the gentry of the country." Having passed Luxor and proceeding towards Esneh, Mr. Combes remarks that,—

"Since we left Djirjeh, when the weather was calm and the sun hot, the numerous sand-banks scattered about in the river were covered with crocodiles. **If** the boats approached them, they would move into the water slowly, and allowing sufficient time to observe them leisurely. At length," he writes, "when we reached Upper Nubia, the Nile was sprinkled with small islands covered with pelicans; on some we perceived monstrous crocodiles asleep, and which awoke at our approach. Often, in the midst of the river, we saw the heads of these formidable amphibia, which would disappear under the waves after inhaling a little air."

We have said enough to prove to our readers, and those hunters whose courage is but ill satisfied with the perilless exploits accomplished in the suburbs of our cities, that for many a year to come game will not be wanting for those who will undertake the enterprise of purging the earth of those monsters which defile and oppress it.

III.—Habits.

CROCODILES live on land and in the water, with a decided preference for the latter. They swim with extreme rapidity, aided by their powerful compressed tail. Nevertheless, all are not equally aquatic. The caymans are less so than the others. The gavials are the most aquatic, a fact which could only be discovered by an inspection of the hind-legs. In the gavial, the toes of the hind-feet are webbed to the tip, and these feet are denticulated the whole length of the external side: they are evidently intended to perform the functions of fins; whereas with the caymans, not only does this denticulation not exist, but the toes are only webbed half their length.

Rivers which overflow, and whose shores are covered with mud, marshy lakes, swampy savannahs—these are their favourite haunts. It is said that the gavial sometimes quits the waters of the Ganges, and will venture almost into the sea.

All are carnivorous and extremely voracious. Livingstone says that they generally seek their prey at·night; Du Chaillu reports that they do so in the morning and evening; but the upshot shows clearly that the crocodilian appetite is equally good at all hours of day or night.

Hidden amongst the aquatic plants or squatting in the mud, at other times motionless on the surface of the water, or floating silently, like the trunks of trees, stranded on the mud, or carried on by the current, they await patiently their prey, or they go to meet it with their jaws extended, their eyes sweeping the liquid expanse and its muddy shores. "One does not see the slightest motion," says Plumier. "We perceive that it has changed its place, but in a manner almost imperceptible, so quiet are its movements; it might then be taken for a piece of floating wood, and I have many times been so deceived." This comparison has presented itself to the minds of Adanson, of La Condamine, and of all travellers who have seen crocodiles in their wild state. Their colour, their elongated form, their immobility, the silence which they keep, deceive their victims. Fish constitute their ordinary diet; as extras they occasionally add any of the animals which come to repose on the water, or to quench their thirst on its shores.

When the saurian perceives its prey it dives, and proceeds under the water towards it, and seizing it by the legs or the muzzle, drags it down to the bottom of the water. To use the words of the missionary just quoted, "the unsuspecting game allows itself to be approached so near that it is snapped up before it has time to spread its wings for flight." Large cattle are not safe from their voracity. "It very rarely happens," says Livingstone, "that a herd of cows crosses the Liambye without some of the young becoming the prey of the monster." M. du Chaillu witnessed the following scene:—As we were paddling along I perceived in the distance ahead a beautiful gazelle looking meditatively into the waters of the lagoon, of which from time to time it took a drink. I stood up to get a

FIGHT BETWEEN THE CAYMAN AND THE JAGUAR.

[*Page* 245.

shot, and we approached with the utmost silence, but just as I raised my gun to fire a crocodile leaped out of the water, and like a flash dived back again with the struggling animal in his powerful jaws. So quickly did the beast take his prey, that though I fired at him I was too late. I do not think my bullet hit him; if it did, it struck some impenetrable part of his mail. I would not have believed that this huge and unwieldy animal could move with such velocity; but the natives told me that the deer often falls a prey to the crocodile. Sometimes he even catches the leopard, but then there is a harder battle than the poor little deer* could make."

In America the cayman will attack the jaguar, which in the New World is the most powerful of his enemies; and a struggle between these two monsters would be a stirring spectacle to witness. The jaguar, knowing the vulnerable place, plunges his claws into the eyes of the reptile; the latter dives, dragging down the jaguar, which, it is said, allows itself to be drowned rather than let go its hold.

Crocodiles do not generally devour large animals until they have drowned them. "The noise they make in eating," says Livingstone, "when once heard, will never be forgotten."

* "Poor little deer!" says the hunter who was preparing to kill him! Talk of crocodiles' tears after that!

Their activity abates during the hottest hours of the day. They then retire amongst the reeds or extend themselves on the sand or in the mud. La Condamine reports that they have been seen sunning themselves on the banks of the Guayaquil and the Amazon for whole days. M. Tremaux, being in Ethiopia, above the cataract of Senadaoui, had the opportunity of examining at leisure a crocodile which was thus taking his siesta extended on the river-bank. "Profiting by his immobility, I had approached him," he says, "under cover of a clump of trees. When my curiosity was satisfied, I walked straight up . to the animal, which, without disturbing itself, slightly raised its great head and appeared scarcely to notice me. I was not a little surprised to see at the bottom of the slope in the bed of the river, and close to the ferocious beast, two donkeys feeding peaceably and quite undisturbed by his proximity. The crocodile, which until that moment had seemed to me not larger than a man, then showed his real size by offering me a point of comparison : he was from eighteen to twenty feet long. Some minutes afterwards the enormous beast slowly glided into the water, lifting one leg after the other in a torpid manner; but no sooner had he reached his favourite element than, with a powerful stroke of his tail, he disappeared like a dart."

It is, in fact, only in this element that they enjoy

the full liberty of movement; but it has been more than once shown that, at least in certain seasons and in certain countries, crocodiles (although less active on the land than in the water) are still capable of moving very quickly on level ground, but in a straight line only, for the short ribs of the neck touching each other prevent these animals from turning easily. Hence there is one chance of safety for those whom they pursue. This knowledge was made use of by an Englishman, who, having at his heels a monstrous crocodile, which had sprung from the lake of Nicaragua, was nearly caught, when the Spaniards who were with him shouted to him to quit the direct path and to run in zigzag. He followed this counsel, and found it valuable.

It rarely happens, according to Livingstone, that the crocodile comes out of the water to seek food. On one occasion, nevertheless, on the banks of the Zouga, he met with one which, although still small (about three feet long), made a dash at his feet, and compelled him to fly in another direction; but the traveller adds, "this is unusual, for I never heard of a similar instance."

These examples, however, are not rare elsewhere. The Count de Forbin, in his "Voyage à Siam," reports that the crocodiles sometimes come close up to the houses at Bancok. La Condamine tells us that the caymans of the Amazon enter the huts of the Indians; and Lacépède reports, that in South America, when the lakes inhabited by caymans become dry, these animals, condemned thenceforward to a terrestrial life, live on game for months together.

It is whilst the crocodile is on land that that extraordinary and charming scene, related by Herodotus, occurs, which has been treated as a fable by moderns, and which was only definitively assigned to science when Geoffroy Saint Hilaire witnessed it during his residence in Egypt.

Whilst the crocodile is going through the water, leeches pass into its gaping mouth, and when on land ants and gnats introduce themselves there. The shortness of its tongue leaves it powerless against these enemies. But a small bird, a plover (*Charadrius Ægyptus*), comes to its aid. The monster opens its mouth, the bird enters, picks the animal's teeth with its beak, cleanses the gums, palate, and tongue, and having performed its task departs.

"The crocodile," says Ælian, "profiting by this service, endures the operation with patience, and remains motionless, so that the plover finds a good meal in the leeches; and the crocodile, rejoicing in its assistance, thinks that he recompenses it sufficiently in allowing it to depart in peace."

In the Antilles another bird (the humming great

renders the same service to the crocodiles of that place as the plover to the common crocodile.

Notwithstanding their voracity, crocodiles can remain for several months without food. Brown, in his "Natural History of Jamaica," reports that he had satisfied himself on this point by tying up the muzzles of several of them with wire.

Some species pass a part of the year in a lethargic sleep. The pike-muzzled cayman, which inhabits South America, and ascends the Mississippi and its affluents as far as the 32nd degree, buries itself in the mud as soon as cold weather comes, and passes the whole winter season in a state of torpor. The rising of the temperature in South America produces the same effect as its falling in North America. At Cayenne and Bahia, in the half-dry marshes, troops of caymans buried in the slime, their backs only visible, await in a lethargic state the return of the rains. Travellers say that some caymans dig holes on the margins of the marshes, into which they retire to sleep the long sleep. Pliny writes, that crocodiles pass the four months of winter in caverns. This was perhaps true of the crocodiles inhabiting the Delta; now-a-days the Nile crocodiles do not become torpid.

All crocodiles are oviparous. The female deposits her eggs, covered with an elastic calcareous shell, in holes, which it digs on the banks of rivers. Livingstone one day made his fire on one of these deserted nests, which was strewed all over with the broken shells. This nest was situated about six yards from the river Zouga, with which it communicated by a broad path. This traveller has seen sixty eggs taken from a single nest. The *cayman à lunettes* of Cayenne, and the common crocodile on the banks of the Nile, deposit a similar number of eggs; the latter lay in February, the others in April. The common crocodile confines itself to simply burying its eggs in the sand; the *cayman à lunettes* deposits them between a double bed of leaves and straw. These eggs are about the same size as those of a goose.

They do not sit on their eggs, although Pliny states the contrary, and pretends even that the male shares with the female the cares of incubation. Solar heat, and in certain cases that which results from the fermentation of vegetable matter massed round the eggs, suffices to bring them to perfection. The female of the common crocodile even abandons her eggs after she has buried them; and at St. Domingo that of the taper-nosed crocodile does the same; but the female of the *cayman à lunettes* (Guinea and Brazil) watches over hers. "She always remains," says M. de la Borde, "at a certain distance from her eggs, which she defends with fury, should any one attempt to touch them."

The eggs of these reptiles have indeed great need

of protection, for they have many enemies. In Egypt the mangouste, in America apes, everywhere water-fowls, and in some places men destroy an immense number. Livingstone reports that the Barotsés and the Bayéyès, tribes of Southern Africa, are very fond of crocodiles' eggs. "They eat the yolk, rejecting the white, which does not coagulate."

"In proportion to the increase of the population," -says this writer, "the nests of these odious reptiles will be more and more sought after, and the species will become less numerous." May it be so!

Lacépède writes, that in America the apes break a very large number of eggs, not merely to eat them, but in some measure apparently for the mere fun of the thing.

Even with the species which abandon their eggs immediately after laying them the cares of maternity are not always confined to nidification. When instinct warns it that its eggs are about to be hatched, the female of the taper-nosed crocodile returns to its nest, unearths its brood, and conducts the young ones to the water.

Lacépède denies this, but he is wrong; the same facts occurred in the countries explored by Livingstone. The negroes even told the latter that the female aids its little ones in coming out of their shells—assistance which, as we shall see, is exceeded by those of the Blue Nile.

"It appeared to me," says Livingstone, "quite needful that their mother should come to their assistance at the time of their birth, for it is a question with them not merely of breaking the membrane with which the shell is lined, but also of digging them out of a bed covered with about four inches of earth."

It is doubtless this last circumstance which necessitates the maternal intervention.

The young go into the water at the instant of their birth. They feed on insects and larvæ; but voracious fishes make great destruction among them, and it is said that the little crocodiles are by no means safe amongst the large ones. During three months the female of the taper-nosed species nourishes and protects its young.

Don Ramon Paez, in his "Travels and Adventures in South and Central America," says: "Despite their great voracity, the mother exhibits some degree of tenderness towards her offspring. Possessed, in this case, of an instinct almost infallible, she returns at a period when incubation is completed, and assists her young in extricating themselves from the shell. Unlike the eggs of birds, crocodiles' eggs are soft and pliable as those of the turtle, yielding, when handled, to the pressure of

the fingers, yet so tough that it is difficult to break
them, and in appearance resembling white parchment.
At the very moment of liberation the young crocodiles
display their savage nature in a wonderful degree,
biting at every object within reach ; the same vicious
propensity is also exhibited by those extricated even
before the completion of incubation. I was once
greatly amused in watching a struggle between two
caricaris and one of these youngsters, not larger than a
good-sized lizard. Each time the birds made a dash
at him, this little saurian, grunting savagely, darted
forward with wide-open jaws, looking for all the world
like a young dragon. During ten minutes the
struggle continued without decided advantage on either
side, when one of the assailants, changing his tactics,
suddenly seized the crocodile by the neck with his
sharp claws, and soared triumphantly with him into
high air. There, loosing his hold, the bird followed
his descent with wonderful rapidity, prepared, when he
reached the ground, to repeat the blow ; but, already
half stunned, the victim soon yielded to superior
cunning."

Catesby, in his " Natural History of Carolina,"
shows us young crocodiles seeking refuge against the
voracity of their elder brethren in the thickest parts of
the marshy forests.

" These aquatic woods are filled with animals which eat each other; half-devoured carcases are seen floating on the water." Lying in ambush on the banks of the lakes and rivers, the tiger in India and the jaguar in America watch the moment when the young saurians approach the shore, seize them with their powerful claws, and devour them.

Livingstone relates, that on arriving one evening on the banks of the Libaye, he put to flight two broods of crocodiles; they were about ten inches in length. Their bodies were marked with alternate brown and pale green bands; their eyes were yellow. When speared, they bit the weapon savagely, yelping all the while like a whelp just beginning to bark.

Added to the testimony of Caillaud, this last fact, reported by a traveller so trustworthy as Livingstone, would suffice to solve the controverted question as to whether crocodiles have a voice. Captain Jobson ("Hist. Gén. des Voy.") assures us that those of the river Gambia, called *bumbos* by the negroes, utter cries which appear to come out of a pit, and which can be heard at a great distance. Catesby reports that the caymans of Carolina, on coming out of their lethargic slumber, make horrible roarings. Bosc, who has visited the same country, says that the caymans make in the evening a frightful hubbub, and that he had frequent opportunities of hearing it. M. de Courdinière, in his " Observations sur le Crocodile de la Louisiane," and M. de la Borde, in the notes already quoted, make analogous depositions. These testimonies cannot be weakened by the otherwise undeniable fact that, during a residence of many years on the banks of the Orinoco, Humboldt, although surrounded every night by crocodiles, never heard the voice of these animals.

Herodotus has stated, with truth, that of all the animals which come out of an egg, the crocodile is of the largest dimensions.

The common crocodile is generally from eighteen to twenty feet in length, but they have been seen nearly forty feet long; the size of the *cayman à lunettes* varies from twelve to fourteen feet, that of the taper-nosed cayman attains the same length. The great gavial of the Ganges is from twenty-five to thirty feet in length, and is said sometimes to exceed forty feet. Their growth is very slow. Aristotle thought that it continued during the whole life of the animal. It is now thought that it continues for twenty years. Viscount de Fontange, Commandant of the island of St. Domingo, kept for twenty-six months some crocodiles which he had seen hatched. Their length was not then more than twenty inches. It is asserted that crocodiles live for a hundred years.

Now let us see the crocodile in his connection with man. On this important point authors show singular differences; possibly we may succeed in bringing them into accord.

CHAPTER XVII.

Crocodiles (*continued*).

IV.—Touching the Ferocity of Crocodiles.

Dampier assumes that caymans never attack man, and that they never make victims, except amongst those who provoke and irritate them. It has frequently happened to him to drink in ponds filled with these animals, and although they were then close to him, they never attempted to injure him.

M. de la Borde says, that in the neighbourhood of Cayenne, the negroes sometimes take caymans five or six feet long, tie their legs, and that the animals suffer themselves to be handled and carried without attempting to bite. From excess of prudence, the jaws are sometimes tied up, or a large metal plate fixed in the mouth. It is better still in some of the rivers of St. Domingo. The pursued animal hides his head and a part of his body in a hole. A slip-knot is fixed to one of his hind feet, and many negroes, pulling at the rope, draw him about, even into the houses, without his exhibiting any desire to defend himself.

Bosc, a traveller in Carolina, agrees with Dampier; he has been quite close to caymans without their making any attempt to bite him.

Audubon goes farther, and says that these animals are so gentle, during the summer and autumn, that the people get on their backs and compel them to carry them.

So much for caymans. Now let us turn to crocodiles. Corneille de Pengu, in his "Voyage aux Indes Orientales," relates that a crocodile was taken sixteen feet and a half in length, and six feet and a half round, which had devoured thirty-two persons, and that on his body being opened, a human skeleton was found therein.

Séba, who reproduced that story, regards it as impossible; and he adds, that the crocodile, far from devouring man, holds him in such fear as to make his escape as soon as he sees or hears him.

Bosman ("Histoire de la Guinée Orientale") agrees with Séba. "They lie in the sun, on the banks of rivers, and the moment they perceive a man, they are so frightened that they precipitate themselves to the bottom of the water." Bosman has never heard of these animals attacking a man, or even a beast.

Thunberg writes: "The presence of crocodiles does not prevent the natives of ·Batavia, as well as the slaves of both sexes, from plunging pell-mell, once or twice a day, into the rivers or canals."

Forbin relates that "the crocodiles sometimes come close up to the houses at Bancok, and as they are very timid, they are easily frightened off by shouting or firing a gun at them, when they immediately escape to the bottom of the water."

The same kind of sport which Audubon describes with the caymans, is practised with the crocodiles on the river Senegambia, San Domingo. According to M. de Brue ("Hist. Gén. des Voyages"), not only do the crocodiles of this river not injure any one, but even "the children can play with them, mount their backs, and beat them, without perceiving any signs of resentment."

Pliny remarks, that the crocodile flies before those who pursue it, and that it permits itself to be guided by men bold enough to leap on its back.

A contemporary traveller, Mr. Combes, writes : "The ferocity of the crocodile has been much exaggerated. I have never seen a boatman hesitate to leap into the water when it was necessary. At almost every turn of our route we saw them up to their waists in the water, endeavouring to disengage their heavily laden barges, which had got aground. And on all sides we saw children coming to fill their pitchers, or to wash themselves, on the banks of the Nile."

Let us not forget the *gavial*. His reputation was never better than that of caymans and crocodiles. Modern travellers have however undertaken to re-establish his character. According to these travellers, the *gavial* never attempts to attack men or animals.

We have heard witnesses for the defence: let us now listen to others.

La Condamine reports that the crocodiles of the Amazon seize the Indians in their huts and in their canoes.

In the Grambo, according to an old traveller, Jobson, the negroes are so suspicious of crocodiles, that they will not venture to swim or wade across rivers frequented by these animals.

We read in the "Description de l'Ile Célèbes (Hist. Gén. des Voyages)," that the crocodiles of the great Macassar river do not confine themselves to making war upon the fish, but that they sometimes assemble in troops at the bottom of the water to await the passage of the small boats, which they stop, and using their tails as hooks, upset them, and then seize the men and animals and drag them into their retreat.

Hasselquist ("Voy. en Palestine") writes, that in Upper Egypt, crocodiles very frequently devour the women who come to carry water from the Nile, and children playing on its banks.

Geoffroy Saint Hilaire reports that it is by no

means rare to meet with Arabs in the Thebaïde, some wanting an arm, and others a leg, which had been carried away by crocodiles.

Listen to Livingstone :—"Every year many victims are made amongst the children who have the imprudence to play on the banks of the Liambye, when they go for water. The crocodile stuns his prey with a blow of his tail, and drags it into the water, where it is soon drowned.

"Fish is the principal food of both small and large, and they are much assisted in catching them by their broad scaly tails. Sometimes an alligator, viewing a man in the water from the opposite bank, rushes across the stream with wonderful agility, as is seen by the high ripple he makes on the surface, caused by his rapid motion at the bottom; but in general they act by stealth, sinking underneath as soon as they see a man. A wounded antelope chased into any of the lagoons in the Barotsé valley, or a man or dog going in for the purpose of bringing out a dead one, is almost sure to be seized, though the alligators may not appear on the surface. After dancing long in the moonlight night, young men run down to the water to wash off the dust, and cool themselves before going to bed, and are thus often carried away. One wonders they are not afraid; but the fact is, they have as little sense of danger impending over them as the hare has when not actually pursued by the hound; and in many rencontres, in which they escape, they had not time to be afraid, and only laugh at the circumstance afterwards: there is a want of calm reflection. In many cases not referred to in this book, I feel more horror now in thinking on dangers I have run, than I did at the time of their occurrence."

He goes on to say, "I never could avoid shuddering on seeing my men swimming across these branches, after one of them had been caught by the thigh and taken below; he, however, retained his full presence of mind, and having a small square raggededged javelin with him when dragged to the bottom, gave the alligator a stab behind the shoulder. The alligator, writhing in pain, left him, and he came out with the deep marks of the reptile's teeth on his thigh."

We have seen that, according to Mr. Combes, the ferocity of the crocodile has been much exaggerated, and he has shown us, in fact, the bargemen going into the water up to their middle, and children filling their pitchers on the banks of the Nile. "Nevertheless," he adds, "accidents are rare, and it is easy to understand that if the inhabitants of Egypt were not satisfied by long experience, they would not show themselves so confiding." This argument would appear to prove little after what Livingstone reports of the improvidence of the *riverains* of the Liambye; and the following fact goes to show the same carelessness on the banks of the Nile, at the same time that it exhibits the crocodile at his work:—

M. Trémeaux was on the Nile, in the eastern Soudan, between Senaar and Lony. Several men were on the sand hauling the boat, when they came upon a hollow filled with water from the river; one of them took the cord in his mouth to swim across the hollow, whilst the rest went round the obstacle. "Suddenly I heard many voices shouting, 'He is seized! he is carried off!' One sailor cried out, 'The crocodile! the crocodile!' a third, 'A gun! bring a gun!' Throwing aside the notes which I was writing, I seized a gun and hurried precipitately from the cabin. Looking to that point of the river to which all eyes were turned, I could only see a circle of undulations, like that which is caused when a body disappears beneath the water. All the haulers were shouting, gesticulating, and advancing cautiously into the water, each pressing against the other, no one daring to detach himself from the group. The doctor extended his hand towards my gun. 'We must make a noise—fire!' said he. I gave him the gun, and seizing a pistol which I had at my belt, we fired. An instant afterwards the man reappeared on the surface of the water, half suffocated, gesticulating painfully, and exhibiting signs of frightful anguish. The wretch was but a few yards in front of the haulers, but not one of them dared to advance to his assistance. The doctor again fired a shot at hazard into the water, to drive away the monster. During this time the boat was rowed quickly towards the poor fellow, and we threw him the end of the cord, which he was still able to seize, and by its aid we drew him on board—one of his legs was crunched!

"The monstrous amphibian, deceived by the floating *ferdah* of the man, had, it appeared, first seized him by the foot, which he raised up, then seizing him a second time by the leg, above the knee, he dragged him underneath the water. It was then that the crocodile—who is as cowardly as he is ferocious—frightened by the detonations of the fire-arms, and by the shouting of the men, had let go his prey.

"The wound was considerable; the articulation of the knee was crushed; the flesh of the thick part of the leg ripped open for a great length, exposing to sight the naked bone. The teeth of the monster had left deep marks. From the foot to the middle of the thigh we counted seven or eight on each side, each of which was sufficiently open to receive three fingers. Others were united by the same rent. A single blow of the powerful jaws of the crocodile appeared to have produced all these wounds."

The poor fellow was carried to land, and remained extended on the sand in the sun, whilst a man went to the neighbouring village in search of some means of transport. Far from complaining, "It was written!" he said, and he thanked God for having saved his life. The boat continued its voyage.

Near there the traveller saw in the sand the remains of a crocodile killed by the natives, who were reproaching it as the cause of the death of many of their friends.

For many hours crocodiles were the subject of conversation of all on board. "Some of our men, who were from Khartoum, stated that the approaches to that city had for some time past become very dangerous, and that many people had perished there. The crocodiles wander near the places where the people come to draw water, and if an isolated person advances too far into the river, in order to get purer water, he runs very great risk."

Among other stories, one is related which is not without analogy with that of the crocodile whose ferocity Séba denied the existence of entirely. Here it is.

" Quite recently a fine tall woman, knowing that the principal victims of the carnivorous monster of the Nile were women and children, thought probably to awe him by her fine and imposing deportment. She walked into the water up to her waist, and there, whilst filling her leathern bottle with the limpid water, she was suddenly upset by a blow from the tail of a crocodile and carried away immediately.

" This event brought a great number of the curious to the banks of the river, and some time afterwards there was seen floating on the water a monstrous crocodile, with a stomach so enormous as to prevent it remaining constantly under the water. Then boats were got together, and they attacked it. The crocodile, in that state, being anything but active, plunged, then soon reappeared on the surface, and as the river was now studded with boats, those who were within reach planted their lances between the openings of his scaly armour. He was soon killed, and they dragged him ashore, and quickly opened him. The animal, by means of his great mouth, which opened to the shoulders, had swallowed his prey whole, and, added the narrators, the victim of this monster had only a few bruises—her wounds were so trifling, that she must have died of suffocation in the crocodile's belly. They hoped even to see her come to life again. With the exception of some of the details," adds

M. Trémeaux, "the foundation of this story seemed to me to be true, for not only was it confirmed by many persons on our boat, but I heard it related in terms almost identical during our last residence at Khartoum."

During that residence the author witnessed another catastrophe, which he reports in the following terms :—

"From the window of the house where we were installed, on the quay, I was occupied in observing the movement of the animated scene in the harbour. A little negro, twelve years of age, had been bought at Kaçane by our *maitre d'hôtel*. This young boy was standing on the edge of our boat. A kind of handkerchief of coloured cotton had just been given to him by his master. Delighted with such a treasure, after examining it minutely, the child shook it in the air. This movement, which attracted my attention, awoke probably also that of a crocodile, for the little *garçon* having let fall his handkerchief into the water, immediately jumped in to regain it, and never reappeared. The water was suddenly agitated, then a series of undulations, which could be seen towards the middle of the river, were for me the only perceptible traces of his being carried away by the crocodile. The sailors who were on the boat, said that they had seen the animal near there, and they recognized on the other shore, where he had gone at once, the agitation produced by his efforts in swallowing his prey."

I must remark, nevertheless, that crocodiles are said not to be able to swallow in the water, and it is so stated by Mr. Milne Edwards in his "Elements of Zoology."

M. Trémeaux relates still, as an eye-witness, an accident which was comic, but which might easily have turned out serious.

"It was near Chendy, on our return. One of the Russians, a servant of Colonel Kovalwski, was sitting on a bank by the river, his legs dangling in the water; he was engaged in washing his feet. All at once he was seen cutting a caper backwards, as if he had been suddenly hurled by a powerful shock. He had described a complete somersault, and found himself sitting on the ground pretty far back. The crocodile had prowled up cunningly, and by slow movements, in front of him. On suddenly perceiving him, the man had not had time to retire. A powerful blow with his tail, by which the monster had endeavoured to throw him into the water, succeeded only in causing him to describe the *pirouette* we saw."

Let us now return to Mr. Combes, according to whom the ferocity of the crocodile has been much exaggerated. This opinion appears to agree badly with the sentiments he expresses in the interesting story we are about to quote.

It was in the desert of Wady Halfa (Lower Nubia). Our traveller was proceeding to Dongolah. It was near the end of the month Ramadan. In the caravan was a Turkish merchant, who wished to procure a sheep, or at least a goat, at any price, which he would have carried on one of his camels, in order to offer it up as a sacrifice at the moment when the crescent should shine forth in the skies. "But," says Mr. Combes, "we were then on the desert side of the Nile, and it would have been necessary to cross over to the opposite shore to find any living animals.

"The Turk went up and down the river, in the hope of discovering some rafts; he shouted to the inhabitants on the opposite shore, but his searching and his cries were vain. He then resorted to the camel-drivers, and promised them a recompense if they would consent to swim across the Nile, and endeavour to bring back a sheep with them. Sobriety is a necessary virtue in the desert, but it was a question of celebrating a feast, and our conductors, like zealous Mussulmans, could not have been better pleased than to be able to comply with the wishes of the pious traveller. Unhappily, crocodiles were numerous in those parts, and in throwing themselves into the river, they would run great risk of being devoured by these terrible animals. This was re-marked to the Turkish merchant, but he, far from being touched by so grave a consideration, proposed a still higher reward, sufficient to tempt the cupidity of the camel-drivers. In spite of the danger which menaced him, one of them, the oldest, suffered him-self to be seduced. He took off his clothes and leaped into the Nile, uttering loud shouts. He was not yet two lengths from the shore, when, towards the middle of the river, a monstrous crocodile elevated his hideous head above the water, and then plunged almost immediately. The swimmer had not perceived the animal, but the apparition had not escaped the anxious looks of the other camel-drivers standing upon the shore. These hastened to call to their companion, signalling the imminence of his danger. We were all in a state of the most cruel anxiety, fearing at each instant to see the rash fellow become the prey of the formidable amphibian. But, thank God! it was not so; at the first warning of the camel-drivers the swimmer turned round, and it was with the most vivid satisfaction that I saw him regain the shore, and he was not slow in securing his safety. He was received jeeringly by the merchant, who perhaps regretted the horrible spectacle which the appearance of the monster seemed to promise us; but, except the merchant, all congratulated the Nubian in having escaped so great a peril. The crocodile reappeared several times on the surface of the river, and allowed himself to float down with the current."

Later, at Khartoum, Mr. Combes was witness of facts which served to convince him that the fears he experienced under the circumstances we are going to relate were by no means without cause; but how can one reconcile these facts with the opinions expressed by him on the nature of the crocodile?

"I was walking," says he, "on the banks of the Blue Nile, whilst many persons were bathing in the river. I was astonished at their imprudence, but the swimmers, assured by their number and the noise which they made, did not seem to experience the least disquietude; nevertheless, at the moment when they least expected it, I heard a great cry, and a man disappeared. The other swimmers, seized with fright, regained the shore with precipitation, and threw into the river whatever they could put their hands on, redoubling their clamour. We were in a state of mortal anxiety, seeking on all sides traces of the man who had disappeared. On looking attentively, we discovered a slight furrow, which cut the river crosswise, and after a moment of cruel suspense, we saw an immense crocodile emerge on the opposite shore, holding in his blood-stained mouth the unfortunate swimmer, who no longer exhibited any sign of life. At this sight the companions of the victim uttered terrible cries, in the hope of compelling the monster to abandon his prey; but the crocodile squatted down on the desert shore, and, scarcely sensible of this tumult, was grinding between his teeth the body extended before him. Some guns had been hastily procured, which were discharged at the ferocious beast; and whether they had any effect, or the monster, frightened by this brisk detonation, wished to shelter himself from a new attack, he plunged into the river, carrying with him the remains of his victim in the presence of a numerous crowd, which had run together from all parts, and which followed in breathless consternation the different phases of this exciting and terrible drama. We remained still for some time on the banks of the river, but the crocodile did not reappear, and we retired in silence."

We have already seen Mr. Combes' argument against the ferocity of the crocodile, in the facts he mentions of the sailors not fearing to go into the Nile, and the women and children taking water and washing therein. What shall we think of this argument when we shall presently see our traveller himself, his mind still filled with the catastrophe which we have just related,

going into the Nile for the pleasure of swimming?
He says :—

"Some days after this cruel event, I myself bathed
in the Nile, with the doctor of Khartoum, his slaves,
and some Turks who had joined us. We had chosen
a safe place, or at all events one so reputed, and in
which it was asserted crocodiles had never shown
themselves ; besides, we had sufficient prudence not
to go far into the river, in order, on the least alarm,
to regain the shore promptly ; and, notwithstanding
the assurances which had been given us, the slaves
threw stones all round us, and kept up a continual
noise, to avert all danger. We had hoped, thanks to
these precautions, that we were safe from any surprise:
unhappily, it was not so. One of our companions,
having had the temerity to advance into the middle
of the stream, was seized by a crocodile, at the very
moment when he was swimming towards us to regain
the shore. He immediately uttered a heartrending
cry, extending his arms in every direction. Notwithstanding the peril which menaced us, we rushed
towards him just in time to seize hold of him, and
to contend with the monster, which was just on the
point of dragging him under. A severe struggle
ensued, and we thought for an instant that we had
come off with a brilliant victory. We had brought
our companion fainting to the shore, but a trail of

blood which he left behind him began to frighten us, and after having got him quite out of the water, we were thunderstruck to perceive that the crocodile had smashed his thigh, and had very nearly succeeded in severing that member from the trunk. The doctor sent his black slaves to the hospital, from which they soon returned with a hand-barrow, on which the wounded man, still in a swoon, was placed. We had him transported to his dwelling, whither we followed him, overwhelmed with sorrow. Notwithstanding the most attentive care, the poor fellow died three days afterwards, a prey to the most poignant suffering."

I have done, as they say at the court, the cause is heard. Enough has been said to form an opinion on the crocodilian family. Before concluding, however, one last fact remains to be established, which will be the object of the following chapter.

V.—On the Possibility of Educating Crocodiles.

The crocodiles brought up in the temples of Egypt allowed themselves to be approached and handled. They were adorned with bracelets and ear-pendants, and, thus decked off, they discreetly took their place in the religious ceremonies. The abundant nourishment

which they received as divinities explains this man-
suetude and familiarity. They willingly permitted
those to open their teeth whose intention they knew
was to fill their mouths.

Aristotle says that the want of food alone renders
crocodiles very dangerous; and what he has said of
crocodiles is true of the whole crocodilian race; there
is nothing ferocious in them but their appetite. For
the rest, except man, I know of no animal (I am
speaking of the superior animals, about which we know
a little) that sheds blood merely for the pleasure of
shedding it; and the tiger himself, in spite of his
wicked reputation, is no exception to this rule.

Aristotle says again, that it is an easy matter to
tame crocodiles, and to do that it is only necessary to
feed them well. Nothing can be more true, and it is
equally true of all members of the family we are discussing. We have a report in the "Histoire Générale
des Voyages" (the responsibility for the truth of which
we leave to that work), that on the shores of the Rio
San Domingo, in Africa, crocodiles are such kind
creatures that the children, who are there badly off for
toys, use the backs of these saurians instead of the
wooden horse, which is not known in that country.
This playful humour on the part of the crocodiles is to
be attributed to the fact that, owing to their generous
nourishment by their fellow-citizens the negroes, they

have yet to learn what is meant by pinching the stomach.

There was at Pompeii, in the Temple of Isis, a painting showing an analogous scene to this which is every day enacted on the banks of the San Domingo. Children are there represented playing with crocodiles. Doubtless it was wished to symbolize the confidence felt in these animals, which, being the objects of worship, found a table always ready served for them in the temples. Imperial Rome saw crocodiles led within its walls by inhabitants of Tentyre (modern Denderah), playing innocently with their guardians.

In some of the primitive countries visited by Cook, tame crocodiles lived in the family with their savage masters. M. de la Borde reported to Lacépède that, at Cayenne, the caymans, fed from the superabundance of a good kitchen, carried their love of peace to such an extent as to leave in safety the turtles placed in the basin where they took their sports. It is said that, at Boutan, in the Moluccas (Spice Islands), they are used as domestic animals and fattened for the table, and that in proportion as they become plump, they become as inoffensive as poodles. At Séba, on the slave coast of Africa, the king of the place keeps in his gardens two tanks filled, not as they are in the basins of the Tuileries, with gold fish, but with crocodiles,—which is not so vulgar.

This negro king, although a barbarian, has the same tastes as some of these ancient masters of the civilized world, whose fortunes were founded by the great man that bore the name of Cæsar; he is likewise on an equal footing with the divine Heliogabalus, who also kept and fed crocodiles, confirming the adage, "birds of a feather flock together."*

All this goes to prove that the crocodilians are not mere machines, that they can remember, and regulate themselves according to circumstances, and can show themselves very different at different times and at different places.

But the change is never so great as to render unrecognizable the portrait, sufficiently true, which Ælian has traced of the crocodilian species whilst painting only that of the crocodile.

The Greek author thus expresses himself:—"The crocodile, naturally timid, wicked, knavish, and very cunning, displays much quickness and subtlety whether it be in carrying off a prey, or in laying a

---

* Scaurus, the edile, was the first Roman who exhibited crocodiles to the people. He showed five. This magnificence was far surpassed afterwards by Augustus, Antoninus, and by the above-named brilliant Emperor. Clement Augustus carried the luxury so far as to bring together into the circus of Flaminius, expressly filled with water, no less than thirty-six crocodiles, on which he let loose a proper number of combatants—unless it were better to say the crocodiles were let loose upon the men.

snare for it. He trembles at every noise, but he fears, above all, the loud shouts of man. In spite of his strength, a bold attack strikes him with terror, &c.

This granted, if we add, or rather if we recollect, that the water is the true element of the crocodile, we shall have, I think, all that is needful to bring into accord the apparently contradictory statements of the travellers and naturalists whose opinions have been reported in the preceding chapter.

VI.—ALL ARE AGREED.

FIRST of all, we must put the gavial aside altogether. It appears certain that he has been defamed by those who have made a cannibal of him. It is sufficient to see his slender snout to be convinced that he could never take such a prey as man. All modern travellers are in opposition to their predecessors on this point, and assure us that they respect man, and have a like regard for large animals. But, in acquitting the gavial, they charge the crocodile. This is the one which is the author of the misdeeds attributed to the gavial.

Ælian had already remarked that in the Ganges there are two kinds of crocodiles, the one gentle and innocent, the other cruel. This remark is correct. The innocent crocodiles are the gavials; the cruel belong to one or other of two species, one of which is the *crocodile à deux arêtes*, the other the crocodile of the marshes, both of which inhabit the Ganges.

The gavials being dismissed, a word on the caymans. Undoubtedly these cannot be absolutely acquitted; but it has, nevertheless, been agreed to regard them as much less dangerous than the crocodiles.

The latter have now principally to be considered. Let us pass on, then, to the crocodiles.

Let us remark, in the first place, that there are several kinds of them. We should be certainly deceived were we to extend to the entire race observations made on such and such a species. There are degrees in everything. One species might be very dangerous to man, and another only slightly. Geoffroy Saint Hilaire thought that there were two species of crocodiles in the Nile—the *Vulgaris* and the *Suchus;* and that opinion, after having been contested by naturalists, has now been adopted by them. Now, according to Geoffroy Saint Hilaire, the *Suchus* has a much more friendly disposition than the common crocodile. Travellers who blacken the characters of the crocodiles of the great river of Macassar, and the Sieur de Bruc, who paint *couleur de rose* those of the Rio San Domingo, make no pretence of describing the whole genus. The first, on the contrary, states that "crocodiles are more dangerous in the Macassar river than in the other great rivers of the East."

And the second writes : "We have observed with astonishment in the river of San Domingo, that the crocodiles,* or caymans, which are generally such terrible animals, are here quite harmless." And Livingstone, referring to those of the Liambye, remarks that "they commit more excesses than those of any other rivers."

Before accusing travellers of contradicting each other on the subject of crocodiles, it is necessary to know if their descriptions apply to the same or to different species. But that is not all, and the most opposite statements might be equally correct, even when applied to individuals of the same species. We will go farther, and say even when applied to the same individual.

One can conceive, in fact, that a traveller would form a totally different idea of a species according to whether he found himself in the neighbourhood of a crocodile famished or satiated.

It is said that at certain times of the year the males of the taper-nosed crocodiles give themselves up to most desperate combats. I imagine that it would be more disadvantageous to encounter them at those periods than at others. And the same may be said

---

* Crocodile is the proper term. America has the monopoly of caymans.

of the female of that species, which takes such good care of her eggs, and watches her young with so much solicitude; she might exhibit quite a different disposition when she has her progeny to nourish and protect, than before she has known or after she has passed the cares of maternity.

There is also a difference between encountering a crocodile on land and in the water; still, no general rule can be established in either of these two cases.

We have seen, in the statements of MM. Combes and Trémeaux, great crocodiles extended in the sun, on the banks of the Nile, gliding into thé river on the approach of man. On the other hand, we must recall that young crocodile in the neighbourhood of the Liambye which put Livingstone to flight. Females leading their newly hatched young to the river, and the crocodiles which, in South America, the drying up of the lakes condemns for several months to lead the life of a terrestrial animal, might be more dangerous on land at those times than when they have only come to enjoy their siesta. Whence it follows that, according to species, place, and season, the man who finds himself on the path of a crocodile, out of his ordinary element, runs a variety of chances; and it is the same if the encounter takes place in the water.

After the accident which happened to the unfortunate hauler who had his thigh broken, the sailors told M. Trémeaux that "the crocodile, when he is on land, never attacks man, and that he always flies at his approach to throw himself into the river, which is his favourite element."

We have just seen that, if that is always true on the banks of the Nile, it is not invariably the same elsewhere. They added that, "even in that element (the water) he does not always attack man;" and that is correct.

In fact, the crocodile can be rendered inoffensive by two methods, either by teaching him to fear man, or by teaching him to love him; if, indeed, the crocodile is susceptible of affection for any living being but those of his own family.

But why not? He knows how to appreciate the services which the plover renders him, and shows his recognition thereof in the crocodilian fashion, by not rendering evil for good. Why should not repeated kindnesses inspire him with the same tolerance towards man? That it should be so with captive crocodiles is a thing neither doubtful nor extraordinary; where the difficulty begins, we agree, is when it becomes a question of explaining by the same cause the presumed meekness of crocodiles enjoying the full liberty of the waves. We have seen, nevertheless, that the traveller De Brue explains

the sweet temper of those of Rio San Domingo
by "the care which the inhabitants take to feed
them and treat them well." I confess that this
explanation does not satisfy me, and that the inhabitants of the Rio appear to me to turn in a vicious
circle. It seems that the feeding and care which
they lavish on the crocodile, by tending to the
multiplication of the species, would have as its result
to give birth to a number of empty, and therefore dangerous, stomachs. For this reason, I
regard as much safer the other method, which
consists in inspiring the crocodile with a wholesome
terror. Its very nature suggests this treatment,
and the effect is unfailing. This great animal
is by no means courageous in proportion to its
size.

Ælian says that it dreads the loud shouts of man.
Of this we have had more than one proof in the
anecdotes already reported.

After mentioning the accident to the hauler, M.
Trémeaux adds: "Our men continued, nevertheless,
to throw themselves into the water, when the necessity arose, as if nothing had happened; to our
observations they replied that there was no danger
so long as they kept close to the boats, or when
men remained in groups in the water." That is

to say, there is no danger when the waters are splashed and a noise is made. This is explained by the cowardice of the crocodile, which by no means invalidates the fact of its voracity.

If gunshots, shouts, and stones cast into the water can intimidate the crocodile, put him to flight, and make him abandon the prey which he has already seized, surely a serious war made upon him would have the effect of curing him of his desire for mischief.

The Tentyrites arrived at this result. "The hunters," says Ælian, "make such a furious war upon them, that the river, cleared of this brigand, flows through the country in profound peace; and the *riverains* trust themselves with safety to swim in its waters, and much enjoy the exercise."

In lieu of cramming the crocodiles, as the people of San Domingo do, or hunting them like the Tentyrites, man sometimes carries his folly even to the extent of regarding crocodiles as gods, and esteems himself honoured in being swallowed by them; and these beasts will never refuse to accord him that distinction. At Ombros, Coptos, and Arsinoé, where this superstition flourished, "one could not with any comfort wash one's feet in the river, draw water, or even walk on the banks, without being always on the look-out."

Wherever man has neglected, or has not had occasion to make his power felt, the crocodile has made frequent victims; and La Condamine thinks that the boldness of those of the Amazon arises from their being so little hunted.

There is still another and last distinction to be made between crocodiles, viz., those which have already eaten a man, and those which are not yet · acquainted with his flavour. Those which have once eaten a man form a taste that way, and become excessively dangerous. The misfortune and shame of our race is, that in many places men devote themselves to giving to the crocodile an appetite for man.

It was told M. Trémeaux that, in certain places inhabited by crocodiles, accidents never happened. But if the monstrous amphibian, by any chance, has tasted human flesh, the place from that time becomes dangerous; for not only has this animal acquired the taste, and lies in wait for his prey, but sometimes others share it with him, and thus become terrible to man. Thus it is always by the same animal or at most by two or three that certain spots of the river are rendered formidable.

Mr. Combes, having reported the sad events of which he had been witness, adds, "An inhabitant of Khartoum, whom I had asked if such accidents frequently occurred, assured me that before the arrival of the

Egyptian troops, that is to say, before the horrors committed by the *defterdah*,* the crocodiles showed but little taste for human flesh, but since the drownings ordered by Mehemet Bey, said the man whom I interrogated, since the Nile has borne the corpses of my brethren, the monsters which inhabit it have become accustomed to a substantial food, which they scarcely knew before, and now we are exposed to imminent danger from swimming in the river, or even from bathing on its shores."

This defterdah, or governor of Soudan, more ferocious, says Mr. Combes, than the tigers and lions with which he loved to surround himself, made sport of the lives of his fellow-men. To cut off the ears of the conquered, and to burn out their eyes with a red-hot iron, were his recreations. Empalement was in constant operation, and the negroes were thrown to the crocodiles in the Nile. There was only wanting to this atrocious man the means of exercising his power on a wider field to have nothing to envy in the celebrity of the most famous successors of Cæsar. Mehemet Ali recalled him at last, but the crocodiles had formed habits which they could not lose in a day, and which,

---

* Mehemet Bey is here referred to ; he had been governor of the Soudan some time before the journey of Mr. Combes.

thanks to the *jellabs*, or slave-merchants, they have probably preserved to the present day. *A propos* of this is one of the scenes related by the traveller we are going to quote. It was in Upper Nubia. Mr. Combes, coming from Khartoum and descending the Nile, had taken his place on board a boat chartered by some jellabs, the cargo being chiefly composed of slaves. Let the witness relate these horrors :—

"A great misfortune had just fallen upon the slaves, already wretched enough ; small-pox had broken out on board, and each day made some victims. We were always crowded one upon another, and in this cruel position the malady spread with fearful rapidity. The jellabs, powerless to arrest the progress of the plague, were compelled to appear resigned, and every time that death snatched from them a slave, they threw him into the Nile, repeating sententiously the words '*Miss Allah !*'—It is the will of God. The sick expired and became cold in the midst of their terrified companions; their masters, under the rule of the most senseless fatalism, made no effort to overcome the terrible effects of the contagion. They stopped less frequently than usual; the dying rested their heads on the knees of those who were yet in good health, and these unfortunates, who were being suffocated by the fever, and who required to breathe free and pure air, passed the great part of the day, and even of the night, in the midst of deleterious miasmas and the most baneful exhalations. Their dead bodies, thrown into the Nile, served to feed the crocodiles, and these famished monsters followed our boat ready to seize the new prey, for which they had not long to wait." This, however, is nothing to what follows:—

" The disease had thrived vigorously for many days, and exhibited no signs of dying out. The jellabs, whose disheartening impassibility had already revolted me, now sometimes showed their ferocity. When the sick were in a desperate state, they did not wait for their last breath, but threw them into the river, where the crocodiles devoured them alive. One cannot form an idea of the sombre grief of the slaves at sight of such horrors. I was myself a prey to inexpressible agitation; and, overcome by my indignation, I loaded the merchants with reproaches, which did not appear to have any effect on them. In their cold-blooded barbarity they could not comprehend my anger; and when I threatened to denounce their unworthy conduct to the local authorities, they replied carelessly, that they were doubtless at liberty to do as they liked with their own property."

After such abominations, one sees the need that the rights of humanity should be protected with an energetic hand.

Mr. Combes had a black servant named Hassan, a very good fellow, but unable to comprehend the gene-

rous fits of anger of his master. "All Europeans,"
he said to me one day, just after I had been reprimand-
ing the jellabs (who never bore me any malice), "take
a lively interest in the slaves. Some years ago I was
in the service of an Englishman who was visiting the
antiquities of Egypt and of the country of the Bara-
brahs. Between the first and second cataract we met
a boat laden with slaves, whom the small-pox was deci-
mating, as in this instance. The English traveller
wished to see them more closely, and he offered a sum
of money to the jellab to allow him to embark with
him. The malady was making fearful ravages; the
slaves were closely packed together, and no time was
lost in throwing the dead bodies, still warm, into the
river to make room for the living. The want of space
contributed to augment the evil. Then when they had
satisfied themselves that a man was mortally attacked,
he was got rid of at once. One case of this kind having
presented itself a little time after the embarkation of
my master, the sufferer was thrown into the river; and,
doubtless roused by the coolness of the water, he uttered
a feeble cry, extending his arms towards us, but he
disappeared almost immediately. The Englishman,
instead of remonstrating with the jellab, threw himself
suddenly upon him, and pitched him, astoundeed as he
was, into the Nile. This jellab was a powerful swimmer, and he soon reappeared on the surface of the river

and made for the boat; but the traveller, far from being disconcerted, took up his double-barrelled gun, and told the swimmer that if he dared to approach he would blow his brains out, and send him to rejoin the wretched slave. The frightened merchant remained for a moment undecided, and seeing the cool and determined air of the Englishman, he thought it prudent to gain the shore and to follow the boat on foot, in the hope that the terrible traveller would soon show himself more reasonable. He rejoined us at the station. The Englishman had grown calm, and returned into his own boat, which was made fast to that of the jellab. He pretended not to pay any attention to the arrival of the merchant; but on the following day, when he was on the point of starting, he went into his boat, and told him that he was going to sail alongside of him until they reached Cairo, and that if he did not treat his slaves with more humanity he should take upon himself to revenge them. We set sail the same time as the jellab, and followed him up to Cairo. In spite of the irritation and anger of their master, the slaves enjoyed some repose, and, thanks to the rough but energetic intervention of the English traveller, none but dead bodies were afterwards thrown to the crocodiles."

Enough of this: let us now see man in his character as the destroyer of monsters.

VII.

NOTWITHSTANDING his thick and hard covering, the crocodile is not invulnerable; that armour has its defects; the weak points are the eyes, the throat, the joints of the fore-legs, and the belly, and with a well-aimed shot the hunter can soon finish him.

One of the three jellabs with whom Mr. Combes was travelling was an excellent shot, and with a common matchlock he had already brought down two pelicans, with which the slaves were regaling themselves. Nevertheless, he had several times exercised his skill in vain against the crocodiles dozing on the islands or floating on the stream; his balls glided off the scales of the saurians almost without disturbing them. At length, a short distance above Carari, he was more fortunate. The wind, which the night before was contrary, had now fallen, and the Nile flowed gently towards the sea. " On the middle of its smooth surface we had seen," says Mr. Combes, " for some minutes an enormous crocodile rising at intervals above the water, his head constantly turned towards us, as if he had been swimming backwards. The jellab who was posted in the prow of the boat watched him attentively, and after having followed and studied his movements, he aimed rapidly at the moment he showed himself and fired: the animal made a somersault and disappeared under the waves, leaving large traces of blood on the water. Our boat, carried along by the current, soon passed the spot where the crocodile had been struck, and we discovered near the shore fresh traces of blood. The pilot turned the prow towards land, and after sailing for half an hour along the shore, we saw the monster extended on the bank and expiring. We landed immediately and hauled him on board."

The negroes in the country watered by the Anengué hunt the crocodile vigorously, sometimes with the gun, but more frequently with a kind of harpoon: they aim near the joints of the fore-legs.

It will be recollected, that when Du Chaillu entered this river the crocodiles were not in the least afraid. The traveller manœuvred his boat so as to isolate the largest of the troop, and lodged a ball in his body in the place we have just indicated. The animal turned over heavily, and after beating the water for a few instants, he sank into the mud. The others turned their stupid eyes towards him for a moment, and then resumed their torpor. The hunter shot a second, which buried itself in the mud like the preceding. They did not take away either one or the other, as the men did not care to go to seek them in the black mud.

Some days afterwards M. du Chaillu took part in a great crocodile hunt. They went in canoes of a very singular construction, quite flat-bottomed, of very light draught, about fifty feet long, and not more than two broad. The oarsmen stand up and handle these boats very ably. Thus equipped, they went into the very midst of the crocodiles. Some were swimming, others basking in the sun on the mud-banks. They took no notice whatever of the boat. M. du Chaillu killed two, one eighteen feet long, the other twenty.

There are in Egypt some people bold enough to swim underneath a crocodile, and stab him in the belly with a poniard: and the negroes of the Senegal do the same. "One Lapot, of Fort St. Louis, amused himself in this way almost every day, and for a long time was very successful, as we read in the 'Voyage of De Brue;' but he at length received such wounds in one of these combats, that had he not been assisted by his companions, he would have lost his life in the jaws of the monster."

At other times, in the same country, the negroes surprise the crocodile in places where there is not sufficient water left for him to swim in, and attack him with a lance, the left arm being protected by a shield of ox-hide. They thrust the lance into the eyes and throat, placing the left arm in his mouth, preventing him from closing it, and holding it open until the animal is suffocated, or until he expires under their blows.

On land they kill them more easily still, **as may be** judged of by the following relation of Adanson :—

"One of my negroes," he writes, "killed a crocodile seven feet long. He had found him asleep in some bushes at the foot of a tree, on the bank of a river; he approached him gently, not to wake him, and very adroitly stabbed him with a knife in the side of the neck, just below the bones of the head and ear, and pierced him almost through and through. The animal, wounded to death, drew himself up painfully and struck the negro's legs with his tail so violently, that it felled him to the earth. But this one, without loosing his hold, rose instantly, and in order to have nothing to fear from the wounded mouth of the animal, he enveloped it in a pair of cotton drawers, whilst his comrade held the tail. The negro then withdrew his knife and separated the head from the trunk."

"In Egypt," says Lacépède, "they dig deep holes on the paths of this inordinate brute, which they cover over with the branches of trees. They are afterwards aroused by the cries of the crocodile, which, taking on its return to the river the same route which it had followed in wandering from its banks, passes over the pit, falls into it, and is at once beaten to death or taken in nets. Others attach one end of a strong cord to a tree; on the other end they fix a hook and a lamb, whose cries attract the crocodile, which, in carrying off the choice bait, swallows the hook also. The more he struggles the farther the hook penetrates the flesh. They follow all his movements, slackening the cord, and wait till he is dead to draw him up from the bottom of the water."

This latter proceeding is the same as that which is employed by the negroes of Carolina, against the caymans, except that they attach the bait and the hook to a tree by an iron chain.

The negroes of Florida join together to the number of ten or twelve, take a large stake, and seizing the moment when the saurian is on the land, they go in front of the beast, and force the stake into his mouth, after which it is not difficult to finish him. Thunberg also reports that the Javanese use baits for the purpose of taking him. "They attach a wooden hook to the end of a cord slightly twisted, and bait it with a piece of carrion. No sooner has the crocodile swallowed this bait, than he struggles uselessly to cut the cord. It gets between his teeth. Besides, the hook which he has in his throat prevents him from closing his mouth, and the hunters, well armed, soon put him to death."

Lastly, the Siamese take the crocodile by two methods, which the Count de Forbin describes in these terms :—" For the first they take a live duck, and under it they attach a piece of wood about six inches

long, proportionately thick, and pointed at both ends.
To this piece of wood they tie a fine but very strong
cord, to which are attached pieces of bamboo, which
serve for floats. They then put the duck in the middle
of the river, and the bird, finding itself embarrassed by
the piece of wood, struggles to get rid of it. The crocodile seeing it, dives into the water, attempts to take
it from below, and seizes instead the piece of wood,
which sticks crosswise in its throat. As soon as they
perceive that he is taken, which is seen by the shaking
of the cord and the agitation of the bamboo, the signal
is given, and the animal is drawn to the top of the
water in spite of the efforts he makes to get free.
When he appears, the fishermen dart their harpoons
into him. These are a kind of dart, the iron point of
which is shaped like an arrow, attached to a handle
about five feet long. To the iron part, which is
pierced in the socket, is attached a very fine cord,
twisted round the stick, which detaches itself from the
iron, and which, floating on the water, indicates the
spot where the animal is. When they have planted a
sufficient number of harpoons in his body, they drag
him ashore and dispatch him with their hatchets.

"There is a second method of taking them. These
animals sometimes come close up to the dwellings.
As they are very timid, there is an endeavour to prevent
them by making a noise, either by shouting or firing

guns. The affrighted crocodile flies for safety towards the water. At once the river is covered with boats, which wait to see him come up to respire, for he cannot remain below longer than half an hour without taking breath. As he rises he opens his great mouth, and then from all sides harpoons are launched at him. If he receives any in his mouth (and the Siamese are very adroit) he is taken. The handle of the harpoon which floats, serves as a signal. He who holds the cord knows when the animal quits the bottom, and wa **as** the fishermen, who do not fail, the moment he reappears, to launch more harpoons at him. When he has received a sufficient number to be dragged to land, they haul him in and cut him to pieces. This second mode of fishing is **more** amusing than the first."

THE END.